CINNAMON

SAMAR YAZBEK is a Syrian writer and journalist, born in Jableh in 1970. She is the author of *A Woman in the Crossfire: Diaries of the Syrian Revolution* for which she won the PEN Pinter International Writer of Courage Prize in 2012 and the Tucholsky Prize from Swedish PEN. She is also the author of several works of fiction in Arabic. *Cinnamon* is her first novel to be translated into English. An outspoken critic of the Assad regime, Yazbek has been deeply involved in the Syrian revolution since it broke out in March 2011. Fearing for the life of her daughter, she was eventually forced to flee her country and now lives in hiding.

EMILY DANBY has worked as a literary translator of Arabic since her time studying the language in Oxford and Damascus. As part of the British Centre for Literary Translation's mentorship scheme, she has worked in collaboration with Marilyn Booth. Emily takes particular interest in the writing of Levantine women and modern Syrian literature.

CINNAMON

SAMAR YAZBEK

Translated into English by Emily Danby

ARABIA BOOKS

This book has been translated with the assistance of the
Sharjah International Book Fair Translation Grant Fund.

First published in Great Britain in 2012 by
Arabia Books
70 Cadogan Place
London SW1X 9AH

Originally published as Rā'iḥat al-Qirfa
by Dar al adab, Beirut, Lebanon

ISBN 978-1-906697-43-3

Typeset in Garamond by MacGuru Ltd

Printed and bound by CPI Group (UK) Ltd, Croydon, CR0 4YY

It was a streak of light!

The door was ajar and, were it not for the light, which streamed from the room in a diagonal streak towards the corridor mirror, then Hanan al-Hashimi would not have noticed the whispers as she trod barefoot along the corridor. She had jumped out of bed, as though something had stung her, having dreamt that she had turned into a five-armed, three-breasted woman.

Hanan was still delirious. She groped at her body, feeling the wine-coloured lace which clung to her chest. She checked for any new limbs or protrusions, not quite convinced that her body had remained in its natural form until she had descended the wooden staircase and hurried to a full-length mirror, which she had rescued from amongst the furniture in the house whose residents had migrated. Hanan knew the mirror would not lie to her; it would reassure her that there were no gaunt, ghastly arms dancing around her body like vipers.

It was just a streak of light!

The jagged streak of light, which bisected the corridor, brought her round from her nightmare. Hanan realised that her feet were bare. She listened to the whispers emanating from her husband's room.

She stopped, frozen. Her eyes bulged. Her feet would not move forward; she could go no further to find out what was going on inside the room – she hadn't been in there for years and couldn't recall its contents. Hanan hadn't the slightest curiosity about the room in which her husband slept; she was simply awaiting his departure.

She approached the mirror and, having turned on the light, stood in front of it, exposed in her short lace gown. As she gazed into the mirror a silly thought flashed through her mind; blind curiosity to know what her husband was up to.

'Have I gone mad?'

Hanan examined her face in the mirror. Her eyes glimmered. She rubbed her thighs, all the while holding her breath. She laughed and was overcome with an instantaneous joy. For a few moments she forgot the noises coming from the room, immersed in pleasure as she stood before the mirror, contemplating her body in all its detail. Hanan hitched up her short gown and examined her buttocks curiously, as though it were another woman's body that she was observing. She groped at the mirror's surface, letting her fingers roam to her face, massaging her cheek. The silkiness of her skin – as smooth as the polished mirror – gave Hanan a feeling of delight. She burst into laughter, then quickly put her palm to her mouth, like a bashful schoolgirl.

Reaching out a hand, she turned off the light, thinking of the shadow she would cast in front of the mirror, finally convinced that her appearance was as it had always been. All of a sudden, she was drowning in darkness. The light streaming from her husband's room had vanished. The door had been pulled shut. She shuddered.

Hanan tried to pull herself together. The only thought in her head was that a thief had broken into the villa. She stifled a scream and dug around in the darkness for the wall, fumbling for safety. Hanan was struggling to breathe and thought about trying to get to the nearest phone; surely her husband wouldn't be awake at this hour and if by some miracle he was, he wouldn't turn off the lights so abruptly at the sound of her footsteps.

Hanan clung tightly to the wall until she had become a part of it. Curling her body into a ball and wrapping her arms around herself, she held her breath. Minutes passed as she stayed huddled. Then, light shone from the room and the whispers returned once more.

Soft whispers. Faint laughter. A tortured moan. Hanan stepped slowly, her footsteps heavy, as she tried to make out the source of the voice. Her body trembled intensely. She stood in front of the door and gripped the handle. Violently, Hanan swung the door open and confronted the scene face-on. The room became a shadowy theatre, illuminated by a dim spot-light. Her face seemed to erupt; the pores of her skin turned into knife blades, protruding like soft pimples, which covered her body from the soles of her feet to the parting of her dishevelled hair.

Her husband lay naked, sprawled on the bed, his face visibly creased in pain. No, not pain exactly. She hadn't seen such an expression before; it rearranged his features. He wasn't himself, yet it *was* her husband; and there, like a deep hollow, in the centre of the dim spotlight was... Aliyah.

This wasn't a dream, was it? She wasn't lying stretched out on her bed covered in sweat on account of her nightmare. It was Aliyah. Aliyah whom she knew better than she knew herself. It *was* her!

It was Aliyah coiling herself seductively around her husband. The moment Aliyah caught sight of her mistress her body froze, yet she continued to stare into Hanan's eyes with piercing intensity. Both remained still as their sight absorbed a sharp ray of light. Glimmering, it settled into the whites of their eyeballs; it pierced the pores of their skin, like the edge of a sword. Neither uttered a sound. Between their two bodies lay that of the husband, alone, humiliated by his own nakedness;

a sight unfamiliar to Hanan. She had spent the whole of their time together believing that he was devoid of any particularities. Even when he was on top of her she felt no pleasure as a woman might in feeling the weight of a man's body on her own; there was nothing more than a heaviness. But now he was naked! Exhausted, he stared into space, apparently unconcerned with what was happening around him. He fixed his hand to a point above his chest and breathed deeply, as though preparing to dive to the depths of an ocean. Hanan's gaze slid quickly over his body. Then, she stared deep into Aliyah's eyes once more. She contemplated the details of Aliyah's body: her dry fingers, which Hanan knew well, blue with cyanosis; her green veins which would shake whenever she attempted to pull apart a limp piece of meat. Hanan took hold of Aliyah's fingers and felt their dryness. Aliyah looked as though she were about to bolt at the start of a long race, crouched over like she might leap from the bed. She didn't dare stand, but sensed her back threatening to give way if she spent another moment in that same position. Air gathered in her lungs. She was afraid that if she breathed out, catastrophe would strike and the walls of the house would tumble down on her head.

Hanan could hear the pounding of her own heart. She breathed loudly, her throat making a rattling sound, almost as though she were choking. She grabbed hold of the side of the bed and took a step forwards. The moment Hanan raised her palm in the air, Aliyah slid under the bed and scampered away like a lizard, the light glimmering in her eyes. She ran towards her room, taking a few short breaths then coughing violently, almost choking.

Hanan stared at her husband's ugly member, dangling like an old rag.

'Aliyah!' she screamed.

She couldn't tell where her voice was coming from – her throat or the pores of her prickling skin? Or did it emanate from the multiple breasts and arms which were now flailing about the room?

It was the taste of unexpected betrayal that prompted her loss of control at that moment. Hanan knocked manically at her servant's door, which was locked from the inside. Panting, she screamed out to Aliyah. Then, with an abrupt change of heart, she decided to get a hold of herself; her fingers stopped pawing at the door and, having ordered her servant sternly to leave, she made her way to her own room.

Hanan locked the door behind her and sat as she tried to control her breathing, which had begun to quicken again. She would wipe Aliyah out of her life once and for all, she decided. It would be as though she had never existed, rubbed out like a word written in faint pencil, ready to be erased swiftly. Hanan heard Aliyah's creeping footsteps in the corridor as she skulked away like a thief. She would wind up back in the dirty little alley she had come from, amongst the piles of tin and the tears of barefoot infants – naked children who would lick their own dribbling noses, and dangle from the rubbish bins like branches of a scorched orange tree.

Hanan felt the relief of someone waking from a nightmare as she heard the screech of the outside gate. All fell silent. Quickly, she moved towards the window. Drawing back the curtains, she peered out tentatively. She followed Aliyah's ghostly silhouette, hoping that it too might be an illusion, like the streak of light. Hanan tried to open the window with her trembling hands, but soon found she had turned to stone. She couldn't bring herself to scream Aliyah's name, nor order her to come back. She had considered it for a moment but had changed her mind immediately. Hanan squeezed herself hard for a second, until her bones creaked and she was sure that she was a living being, made of flesh and blood.

In the blue dawn, Hanan continued to follow Aliyah's figure. She sent her gaze to the horizon, where flocks of strange birds appeared, as though gathering to bid farewell to the little one as she stumbled on her way. After Aliyah's figure had vanished, Hanan shut the curtains and slipped into bed, taking in the scent of the previous night's bed sheets: the scent of cinnamon.

~

It was the streak of light!

It was the light which would drown Aliyah's nights in darkness when she forgot to lock her mistress's door, before stealing down from the top floor to the master's bedroom.

As Hanan al-Hashimi descended the stairs, Aliyah was trembling with fear. She imagined that her mistress had followed her and caught her, discovering the truth at last. Aliyah froze, expecting the door to open and allow her a glimpse of the shadow which stirred on the other side. Her hand turned dry and rigid and she lowered her weight off her master's body. Collapsing beside him, she was still unable to prise her stiff fingers from his member. She thought about jumping from the window, or hiding under the bed, but found herself paralysed, as if in a dream. The streak of light was the truth which prompted her to scurry like a lizard from under Hanan al-Hashimi's feet.

Aliyah was startled by her own movements: how had she soared like that from the master's bed to her room? The moment her head hit the floor she thought herself in a nightmare, dropping into a bottomless chasm. Yet the sound of approaching footsteps convinced her that this was the waking world, and as the mistress began pounding against the carefully locked door, she stirred completely. Aliyah knew that the time for games was over, that her mistress wanted to rip her to shreds between her jaws. She could hear the sound of her teeth grinding, like the grating of a rusty lock. Hanan sobbed like a child, her words to Aliyah coming out in a scream: 'You dirty pimple-faced beggar!'

Before she had put on her night gown and had moved from her mistress's room to her own, as Hanan al-Hashimi had ordered, Aliyah remembered how Hanan's eyes had brimmed with love and contentment, how a secret delight had taken hold of her body and transformed it into a mass of delicious shudders.

But now, she was a foul scrounger. How had it come to this? How had those beautiful eyes turned to flame? Aliyah's lips quivered as she gathered her clothes, whilst the scent of a strange chill wafted from her limbs. It was a peculiar coldness in the midst of a blazing summer, when salty droplets of sweat trickle over the skin. Her body shivered at an icy sensation, provoked by the images in her delirious mind – pictures culled from tales of death, of dying from the cold, in the middle of an empty street, on a grimy pavement.

And so, Aliyah would spend her days dreaming of the nighttime which would make her queen. She contemplated the night's special qualities, the things about it which she loved, for which she waited. Night was when her mistress would call for her, after she had returned from one of her soirées. Night was her ally, able to touch the passions of her heart.

As the first half of the night began, Aliyah would take hold of her sceptre, touching the invisible crown of her power before briefly falling asleep. When she awoke she would doze in her bed once more, ready for the mistress's summons.

In the second half of the night, she would slip down to the master's bedroom and lie naked beside him, sleepily toying with his soft flesh, before abandoning him for her own room. He wouldn't grumble when her games failed to return his manhood, and Aliyah was never concerned by her failure; she preferred to lie in his arms and listen to his hot breath... Each time, a little before the break of dawn, she would return to her room, wash, then sleep like the dead, knowing that the daytime was approaching, that her magic cloak would soon be stripped from her and she would be obliged to take orders once more.

Aliyah had not realised that the streak of light, which she had neglected out of carelessness, would reduce her queendom to ruins. She hadn't needed much cunning to keep her place on the throne, having picked up a few life skills and learnt how to dominate in the bedroom. It had never occurred to her that in the dead of night, her mistress might wander down to the room on the ground floor, when she had left her deep in sleep.

The moment Aliyah caught sight of the sparks in her mistress's eyes, her mind leapt upon memories of a certain fear and the feeling came back to her in its entirety. It was a fear of something unknown, something she was completely unable to identify, even though a taste of anxiety had for a long time nestled inside her. There had always been a veil separating her from it – a fine, fragile membrane which would not grow more robust with the trials of the years ahead. It was buried at the deepest point of her heart and, although the passing of time drew her further away from the world of her child-hood, time could not erase her anxious shivers, or her violent facial spasms, which Hanan al-Hashimi considered amongst Aliyah's attractive qualities. They were the same spasms which, in a matter of moments, could become tremors of fear, making her face muscles twitch cruelly. Her right cheek would rise and the left would fall, her parted lips revealing small teeth. Then, she would bite down on her lips, her eyes quivering as she tried to stop the streaming tears, feeling as if she were suffocating.

In that fleeting stretch of time as she scarpered to her room – a few moments, which felt like a hundred years – Aliyah thought back to how the light had vanished from her eyes, how, naked, she had bolted from the old man's bedroom and felt herself falling into an abyss. She locked the door, dropped to the floor and broke into tears, which were halted only by the sound of Hanan al-Hashimi's voice ordering her to leave.

Aliyah imagined that, were she to leave her room and throw herself into her mistress's arms, she could turn the magic on the magician and appease Hanan. It was still night and morning was not about to break just yet; she was still the only queen. Yet, when day did come and she became a servant once more it would be another matter. Her faith in the magical powers of night gave her confidence that she could do it, but the malice she had recognised in her mistress's eyes held her back. Quietly, she picked up her bag and left the villa without looking back. As she left the house, Aliyah was unaware that Hanan al-Hashimi had not moved from behind the window.

≈

The streak of light: it fashioned signposts that sent Hanan into the void, compelling her to bid farewell to Aliyah's silhouette as she stood behind the curtain, her eyes wide open like dark cave entrances. Hanan pressed her hand hard into her shoulders until she heard her bones crack, wanting to be sure that she wasn't dreaming. Then she slipped into bed, certain that she would wake up in a better frame of mind.

Yet the streak of light appeared in her nightmares too, as a whip of flames which flogged her body until her flesh was in tatters and her bones jutted outward. The streak was a fiery snake, crawling out from the gap in the open door and finishing up at Aliyah's head. The girl was holding a limp piece of meat between the husband's thighs, which grew until it became a viper that she rode upon as it sprouted wings and began to fly in circles, flapping in Hanan's face.

Hanan woke up from the nightmare. She sprang from the bed again as though stung and peered at the curtains. Perhaps it was all a nightmare – the whole thing simply conjured up in her troubled dreams! Hanan murmured to herself, waving her hands in the air to ward off any spirits. She felt as though she had slept for a thousand years, although she knew it couldn't have been more than an hour. She rushed to her mirror.

'I won't let this petrify me. These horrible limbs will soon disappear; they'll stop growing any moment. All I have to do is get a hold of myself… Right, you stupid bitch?' She struck out at the wide mirror on the wall.

'Where have you been all this time?' said a voice.

'I am the Mirror, and which one of us knows the other better than the other knows herself? Quick, we've only a few moments to talk.'

'I know I'm imagining things. It's all a dream. No, not a dream; it's just my subconscious showing itself to me for a while.' Hanan told herself, preening before the mirror. She perched on the edge of the bed, gazing into the mirror's smooth surface as though searching in some far-off place for someone unfamiliar.

'I didn't throw her out! I couldn't possibly have thrown her out! She's still asleep in her room. She's waiting for daylight, to start work.'

Hanan whacked the mirror. She stared into the two piercing eyes which glared back at her.

'I haven't even left my room! They're just images! Images rotating in my exhausted brain,' she said, shaking her head violently.

Hanan slapped her chest and pursed her lips. She groped at her arms and breasts, then grabbed the mirror on both sides, clasped it in her arms and shouted, 'He's still snoring, the old crocodile. There's no way she'd even go near him, never mind wrap herself around him like that. She couldn't have made herself get anywhere near his cold body, could she?'

She moved away from the mirror, lit a cigarette and drew back the curtain, watching the birds as their shapes changed and they became tiny, multi-coloured specks. A few white clouds made various shapes in the sky. For a moment she imagined there was someone watching her, sitting atop the clouds. Hanan closed the curtain and jumped onto the bed. After steadying her feet, she stared recklessly into the mirror, where another woman appeared, her appearance much like Hanan's. The woman whispered to her, hissing almost:

'You're lying to yourself though, aren't you? You're jealous of her – a lowly servant, a nobody. She's got you talking to yourself. Who gets jealous of a skinny, low-life servant who fucks an old man, who devours his dick like a... like a whore?

She's eating away at your insides. She's eating away at you like a maggot, sucking dry the sweetness inside of you.'

Hanan sobbed. 'I just want to hold her close to me!' she cried out, her voice hoarse. Her skin itched. She groped at her thighs and tugged hard at her hair, yelping in pain. Imagining a voice calling her, Hanan bounded towards the window. She drew back the curtains and opened the window. Eyes loomed amongst the clouds, peering down at her. She shut the curtain again and inhaled the scent of her bed sheets.

'Are you mad? You saw her with your own eyes. She was in his bed. It's just your subconscious, you stupid bitch. You know what the subconscious can do to a woman disturbed by the unsightly things she's witnessed.'

'But I didn't see anything unsightly. Aliyah is so slight, so soft and she's got no one to turn to now. She'll have to live on the streets.'

'She's just a pair of hands. Replace her!' screamed the other woman from inside the mirror.

Hanan stopped on the tips of her toes, pulling at her hair and shuddering. She tried to close her mouth so that she could no longer hear the words coming from her own voice. She clung to the mirror, concealing the ghostly figure with her palms.

Hanan retreated from the mirror and hid in her bed, curling her body up into a ball and pulling the covers over her head. Her eyes remained open, staring back from the mirror. Closing them, she began sobbing, her body shaking. She stopped up her ears with the sheets but the voice grew louder.

'It wasn't a dream. Run downstairs – his flesh is covered with the traces of her saliva; the imprint of her lips is all over his skin. Look at yourself, you miserable wretch! Cry all you want, your days have turned to nightmares!'

Hanan threw the covers onto the floor and jumped up on the bed. She stood upright on the mattress, fell and attempted to get up again. In an instant, the bed seemed to become a pool of moving sand and she could barely get her footing before it quaked under her feet and she was on her knees again.

'Don't say a word,' the mirror threatened. 'Don't talk to me about torment; I know it far better than you. I keep it stored away here in its velvet boxes. Look at me. Press on my heart, then you'll know. Do it, before I break you; before I reduce you to splinters. Do you really think you are a living, breathing being? You're nothing but emptiness and thin air. You never even existed. But if you just do the right thing, you can be free of your agonies. All you have to do is stick the blade into your heart. Isn't it enticing? Go on, do it.'

Hanan struck out at her heart in the mirror and gave a loud laugh, delight sketching its way across her face. Suddenly she frowned and pressed her lips together.

'I won't do it. I'm not sure of anything.'

'Liar! You're lying. Ever since you were a little girl, you've lied and faked those pallid smiles, so that everyone would gather round you and applaud. And now where's it got you? Prisoner to a dirty little maid.'

'I'm begging you, get away from me! Why are your eyes so yellow? And why is your hair a mass of monstrous snakes?'

Hanan finally stood up from the pool of shifting sand and took a few heavy steps. She felt like a tiny ant. Everything around her grew longer and wider: the bed was the size of a train, the mirror as big as the sky and the ground below was a pit which she fell deeper into with every step, unable to keep upright. She began to tremble hard, shaking uncontrollably.

Hanan collapsed onto the mattress.

'I can't do it. I miss her! Why did I throw her out like that? Had I lost my mind? Maybe she'll come back. She'll knock on the door in a few minutes, for sure. She's got nowhere to go, nowhere very far from me.'

'Go on then, burn in your own hell; it'll eat you up and make her the new mistress of the household. You won't even know who you are then.'

Hanan jumped up once more, then struck the mirror, which gave out a loud noise, accompanying the howling wind as it sent the curtains flying into the room. Such a morning wind in the heart of summer seemed strange, she thought.

'You're lying. You know I've never asked for anything from life. I just want her to come back.'

As Hanan sat on the floor, out of the mirror there stepped an old woman whose appearance was much like her own. It was her mother, emerging from the depths, scowling straight at her daughter. Frightened, Hanan pulled the sheets over her head once more just as Aliyah had done as she fled the streak of light.

Hanan heard the howl of the wind once more and her mother vanished with the billowing curtains.

Every now and then, Aliyah looked back towards her mistress's window, hoping it would open suddenly, Hanan waving out, calling her to return. But the window stayed shut, and her high heels were of little use in helping her to walk steadily.

Aliyah felt the cold make her skin quiver. Her bag was heavy. She wasn't sure exactly what she had thrown inside before leaving. She remembered slipping the photograph in first – a faded photograph with tattered edges – and four old volumes of her favourite title: *A Thousand and One Nights*. Aliyah had never forgotten the name in all of the years she had spent in her mistress's service. She had stolen the book by stealth, after she had been forbidden to enter the library; from it she had learnt how to draw the stories in pictures. She called the book 'the grandmother' after the television had shown her the power of grandmothers to turn their tasks into acts of domestic magic when they told stories to their grandchildren. Aliyah would dream that she was a spoilt granddaughter, whose grandmother would put on her gold-rimmed reading glasses, sit next to her copper-framed bed and tell her stories. In the middle of the night, she turned her fantasy to reality.

This dream had prompted Aliyah to create a little theatre on her bed. She would hold the book, sitting dignified, like a grandmother. Then, putting on the glasses which she had stolen from her mistress's chest of drawers, she would gently clear her throat and read, her voice soft but clear. The glasses caused a few problems; they were sunglasses, with dark lenses which made it difficult to read. So that the tinted lenses wouldn't obstruct her view, Aliyah pushed the glasses to the end of her nose. Then she would read, pausing between passages to look to her left and talk to her imaginary granddaughter Aliyah. After they had finished their conversation, she would put the book aside, lie down and plead with her grandmother not to stop reading until the night was over and Scheherazade saw the light of day. Aliyah had memorised all of the stories in the book and knew all of the characters. She would weep for the beautiful princesses and for the lovers and, day by day, she became ever more infatuated with the heroine. She longed to act like Scheherazade, if only there were someone who'd take notice!

Aliyah no longer just narrated the stories; she had become talented at drawing them and acting them out. Sometimes she would mutter the spells she had memorised to ward off evil spirits and keep herself safe. She would play the wicked sorceress, guarding a sullen expression throughout the day as she peered at those around her with apprehension and suspicion. Every now and then, Aliyah would exhale all of the air from her lungs in one great breath, like a dragon. This, amongst other things, made the cook keep her distance; she swore to her husband that the filthy, black servant girl was mad, that she'd been possessed by the Djinn.

The book became Aliyah's secret garden. She couldn't bear to leave it behind, even though it was heavy and the pages were tattered, even though she was afraid that the master and mistress would accuse her of theft. It didn't matter; she would take it with her. She wrapped it up in a few shirts and tossed it into the bottom of her bag. On top of the book she put her drawings of the stories she had memorised, which she had stored secretly, along with the red velvet, gold-rimmed notebook. Aliyah had held on to the notebook ever since she had started to keep a diary of her days in the house, realising too how important it was that she put her memories of the district of al-Raml down in writing. The idea came to her as she sat in the beautiful library, where she had taken to spending whatever hours remained of the day. The library, which opened onto a spacious balcony, was home to Hanan and Anwar's hundreds of books of different types and sizes.

Aliyah had started to toy with the books as she cleaned the library. With the days that passed she read more and more of them, until the master and mistress realised that the servant girl, who disappeared towards the end of every day, was gnawing at the books like a mouse. After that, they forbade her from loitering in the library, so Aliyah resorted to trickery, carrying a book beneath her dress and going upstairs, then locking herself in her room to devour it with delight. In the morning she would return it in just the same way.

Aliyah began writing down everything that happened to her, keeping a diary in the velvet notebook which she had stolen from amongst the books. It was that same notebook which she stroked against her cheek during the many lonely evenings she spent waiting for her mother, imagining that the touch of soft velvet against her cheek was similar to the joy she would feel well up inside her the moment she caught sight of her mother's faint smile.

After placing the tattered photograph inside the velvet cover, Aliyah had begun to stuff her bag at random with whatever was within her reach: pieces of jewellery that her mistress had brought her from Beirut and the embroidered chiffon night-dresses filling her wardrobe. As she wrestled with her possessions it dawned on her that, besides the clothes for sleeping or for housework which filled her wardrobe, all she owned was a pair of blue jeans and a white shirt.

From this load which weighed her down, it was the tattered photograph that Aliyah wanted to hold onto more than anything else. The photograph was the only material evidence she had to prove that she was not born from nothing, that once upon a time she had belonged to a family, even if she had stubbornly lived her life in her imagination.

Aliyah brought back to mind everything she could see in the photograph, particularly the piece of chocolate. She prodded at the bag, then came to a stand-still and looked back. The window seemed smaller than it had done a few minutes before.

Sitting under a tree close beside a marble wall she held her bag in her lap. Opening the bag, she decided to rest a little while longer. Perhaps her mistress would change her mind and open her window.

Aliyah started to toy with her belongings again. She pulled the photograph out and held it carefully in her hands. In the first light of dawn, the picture seemed coloured ashen blue and dark yellow, but it was still the same image. She held it with quivering fingers, waiting for any sign of movement from the closed window.

She examined her position in the photograph, tucked in amongst her family. Still only four years old, she was dark-skinned – pitch black in fact – and wearing a woollen smock which only partially covered her tiny body, leaving her ankles exposed and her stomach to protrude where the garment had begun to fray in the middle. Her dark-brown trousers did not conceal her midriff; too wide for her skinny waist, they left one side exposed, whilst the other was concealed only by the skinny, bony figures whom she pressed up against. Everyone in the photograph was staring into the camera: Aliyah, her five brothers and sisters, her father and mother. Whoever saw them couldn't fail to notice the blank astonishment on their faces. Aliyah recalled that this was the only photograph ever taken of her family. It was taken by a journalist wandering in the alley-ways, flashing her camera, bestowing her smile here and there and buying chocolate for the children.

The memory had never left her, not because of the chocolate, which she never got to taste, or because of the photograph; it was the agonising beating she had received from her father which was unforgettable. That evening, the children had followed the journalist, laughing for her and then running away, burying themselves in their mothers' laps whenever she approached. The journalist peered gormlessly at the women's pregnant bellies and the scrawny children cowering between their legs or hiding in their mothers' arms.

Aliyah pulled at her hair, twirling her curly locks nervously as she peered at the journalist's blonde mane. Every now and then she jumped up, trying to touch it. It was the first time she had ever seen a white woman's hair; in all her four years, she had never been beyond the neighbourhood alleyways. Aliyah imagined that after a few minutes the lady would go plant herself in their neighbour's house, where there was a small television. Then she would climb into the television and become a plastic toy or maybe a cartoon show.

Her piercing gaze, the gleaming white around her two black pupils and her flushed complexion gave the journalist the appearance of a small wild animal. The children around her were afraid to hassle her, fearing the deep scratches she would engrave on one of their faces – whichever one dared to pounce on her.

Alone in the blue morning twilight, Aliyah recalled the day that the picture was taken. She had managed to get hold of quite a handful of chocolate and the other children had crowded around her, trying to steal it. She slipped away from them but they followed, and when they caught up a quarrel broke out. The quarrel ended only when they had all received a clout around the head from their mothers, who cursed the blonde woman for disturbing their day as they tried to break up the fight. By the time Aliyah returned, the chocolate had been trampled by the gang while attempting to snatch it from one another. Nobody got what they wanted; the chocolate had turned to a sticky goo which soiled their clothes even more, and the children could do nothing but stick out their tongues to lick the faint traces of chocolate from their fingers.

Daytime had drawn to an end and the children were tired from running and jumping about. Most snuck from their houses to the graveyard to smoke the cigarettes, or the stubs, which they had gleaned along with the remnants of any goods left by living souls visiting their dead.

The graveyard was where the neighbourhood boys hid their secrets; it was their kingdom, which they divided in their own way. Occasionally, they would let a few of the girls hang around, usually their confidants, who would smoke with them and share in their plots against the boys of other neighbourhoods. Aliyah was one of the girls not trusted with the graveyard's secrets; she wouldn't smoke the boys' cigarette stubs or let them feel her backside and she took no pleasure in cleaning around the graves before the boys, who got to keep the hoarded goods, arrived. For these reasons, a large faction of the boys held a grudge against Aliyah and, as she ran away panting, they saw a suitable opportunity to attack. The chocolate in her hands was squandered. Aliyah stuck out her tongue and lapped up what she could of the melted remains, which had mingled with the snot running down towards her mouth. She gulped for air, swallowing her own mucus and never came to the sweet taste of chocolate.

Darkness grew thick in the neighbourhoods illuminated by nothing but a dim glow coming from the small windows, and most of the girls got scared, disappearing into their houses. There were two girls who would assist Aliyah in her many brawls with the boys. The first, a year older than herself, resembled a mouse: small, with slender limbs, a round belly and protruding teeth. When they got into fights, the girl would clutch at Aliyah's hand before jumping on the boys' backs and twisting round to bite them on the behind. The second girl was tall, with the wizened palms of an old man. Although still very young, she would accompany her sister to work in the houses, returning each time with a stash of precious objects which she stored away in her breast pocket: sweetmeats, rubber sweets – as she called them – toy soldiers, a single doll's shoe, a colourful hair comb, plastic roses. The flowers, which she stole from the grand sitting-rooms, would be used to decorate the window in their home.

The two girls would encompass Aliyah like a binding rope, spitting straight at the boys who would lower their hands in obscene gestures to the level of the girls' thighs. This always sent the girls crazy, and they would hurl back even cruder insults. But this time, when they heard the angry male voices the girls fled, leaving Aliyah to confront the boys alone. They had encircled her and were determined to get hold of what she had in her fist. Aliyah scarpered once more, darting through the alleyways. But before she could work out where she was, the boys jumped on her from behind. While one grabbed her by the hair, another plunged his teeth into her clasped hand, which she opened as the third boy twisted her arm. After prolonging the torture for some time, the boys were surprised to discover that Aliyah wasn't holding the chocolate. All they found in her clenched fist was a sour taste, which lingered on their tongues when they attempted to lick her palm. The boys started to spit at her, kicking her and cursing her. To begin with, Aliyah remained calm and surrendered, but as soon as she'd scampered far enough away, she gestured with her fingers towards their backsides, cursing their mothers and the dirty place from which they had been born.

'Only a real man can catch me!' Aliyah began to shout. This was enough to set the boys off. They chased her, hurling threats as she leapt away, aided by her slender frame and her familiarity with the alleyways' twists and turns. She was heading for home, to get to safety before they could catch her. She didn't notice when one of the boys was dragged off the street by his mother, who scolded him and grabbed him by the hand to pull him inside. As the darkness grew stronger, the two remaining boys started to get scared. Black cats with fluorescent eyes scaled the walls as the light faded into total darkness. In the narrow alleyways, the wind whistled a ghostly tune. Yet the boys did not turn back because, every now and then, Aliyah glanced back at them and gestured at their backsides. She was burning with rage for having been deprived of the foreign chocolate, a taste she had never known in all her life.

The clatter of tin roofs and the noise of miauling cats grew louder, and a light rain began to fall. Aliyah had reached the top of the alleyway leading to the room where she lived with her family. She relaxed her pace and waited, but it was only a few moments before her enemies appeared, coming to a halt before her. Aliyah panted like a puppy, resting her hands on her hips as she stared straight at the two boys in defiance. The boys prowled in circles around her, having decided that variety would be their tactic in torturing her. Meanwhile, Aliyah's thoughts were on one thing alone: to pounce on one of the boys' backs and cling on, then bite him on the neck. She had seen cats do it and had once tried it out successfully on the boys, who had begun to fear her after that.

Aliyah slipped from under one of the boys' legs and jumped on his back. She ripped his shirt and plunged her teeth into his neck, until he started to scream. The second boy pulled her hair, but she clung to the other's back, her body becoming an extension of his as he shrieked. This brought the neighbours outside. The sight of the little girl suspended from the boy's neck was a sight for them all. Aliyah closed her eyes, tensed her limbs and wrapped her thighs around his waist. Were it not for the screams of the gathering crowd – the boy's mother in particular, who screeched as she lashed out at the girl – then Aliyah would have clung on longer. Despite what was happening around her, she kept her eyes closed. Suddenly she jumped back; it was clear now that things had gone too far when the grown-ups had interfered, but by the time Aliyah had retreated the news had already overtaken her and found its way to her home. She was swept along by the crowd – the boys' families and the neighbours – who knocked on the door to the little room, causing the tin roof-sheets to shake over the heads of her family.

With a shiver, Aliyah woke up. Looking out towards the horizon, there was nothing but clouds defying the sun to rise from beneath them. In the other direction, not far from the wall which she rested her back against, the window was still closed. Aliyah contemplated the photograph a long while, before putting it back in her bag with a sigh. She shut the bag once more, her teeth beginning to chatter with the cold again. Aliyah picked herself up, grabbed hold of her bag and carried on her way.

∼

That streak of light – it dropped down from the mirror towards the stone floor, covering it with tiny images of light. Each image emitted a slanted beam and every beam transformed into a different face, crowding around Hanan's bed. Hanan searched among the faces for Aliyah, attempting to recover her scent, now faded from the room. What had Aliyah been like? Could she recollect that first glimmer in her eyes? Had she any memory of the girl other than her petrified glances just now?

Was it a long time ago, when her heart had pounded for the violence she saw in the girl's eyes?

It had been a red autumn day when Aliyah entered the one-story building in Muhajireen, precisely seven years ago. Hanan al-Hashimi was sitting on a wine-coloured sofa embroidered with gold, in a style like damascene brocade. Her lips trembled as she struggled to listen to the swarthy man holding Aliyah by the hand. The man spoke to Hanan in a coarse, yet deferential, voice about the arrangement they had made on the phone a few days ago.

'I don't want Aliyah going out alone, ma'am,' he stammered, turning his face away. Hanan looked at him, her eyes drifting and dulling slightly, before she opened them startlingly wide, staring at the little girl.

'The hijab,' the father said, pointing at Aliyah's head.

As she looked at the girl, Hanan realised that her head was wrapped in a faded yellow rag, fastened near the top of her ear with a flower hairpin.

'I don't want her taking her headscarf off outside your house.'

Mistress Hanan signalled her agreement before exiting the spacious room, where the walls were adorned with works of stained glass and mother-of-pearl inlay. She would recall his instructions in the years to come and find them very strange, for neither he nor any other member of Aliyah's family ever showed their faces again. It would seem even more peculiar to her that Aliyah never mentioned them. Even when Hanan tried to ask her about her mother – a situation which arose repeatedly in their many years together – the little girl would respond with a shake of the head, or by simply lowering her gaze.

That red autumn afternoon, as the father stood issuing instructions on his daughter's hijab, Hanan exited the sitting room abruptly, leaving them alone together. Aliyah was waiting for him to vanish, to discover what sort of a future fate had chosen for her. All the while she was goaded by the image of her mother crying. She would have preferred anything at that moment – anything at all – to being in the company of that man, who made a periodic appearance at the house to take the money that was meant to feed her and her siblings, who had killed her sister and would kill her too one day, for sure.

Aliyah had no idea that this mistress, who spoke with clear disdain, would prohibit her even from going out alone and would determine the course of her life as the fancy took her. The mistress left Aliyah's father and went to her husband's room. 'The maid is here with her feral father,' she told him, taking a large sum of money from the metal safe tucked away in the deepest corner of the room. Hanan had felt a deep sense of confusion as she examined the child's face, which was framed with sandy yellow. Within a week that dark little face would have turned a flushed crimson. It would take some training, she realised, before the girl could manage the responsibilities of the new villa where she was about to move with her husband.

Hanan felt quite bewildered, her fingers trembling as she registered her husband's disinterest and retreated from his room. Frustrated, she stamped her feet hard against the floor. She knew it, he really was just like a crocodile; she had known it in every minute spent in his vicinity. His only human feature in which she found no animal resemblance was his voice; it was more the soft, shy voice of a child, barely even audible.

Hanan told her husband about the maid and waited for his reply, for the sound of his voice to calm her as it usually did. But he remained silent, his form settling into its usual repulsiveness. Hanan left and went to the sitting room, where she handed the father an envelope. The father stood up eagerly and began counting the money; Aliyah watched his expression as the mistress waited for him to leave. Moistening his finger with the tip of his tongue, he took a deep breath then started again, turning the notes over in his hands.

An elderly servant entered the room carrying two glasses of juice. The servant peered at the man curiously, disgusted by his black nails. He looked at the child, then at his mistress, who understood his expression and was reminded of how long it would take to arrange her new life with this girl in her service. Meanwhile, the girl was captivated by the works of art on the wall. She contemplated the paintings and the artefacts in the strange house, most of which were more than half a century old.

Aliyah's father finished counting his money and shook the mistress's hand respectfully, bowing slightly. He inclined further to kiss his daughter, who shuddered and backed away from him. It was the first time he had ever kissed her; the first and the last. The mistress granted him permission to visit his daughter on occasion and would allow the rest of her family to come too, not knowing that he wouldn't be returning to the family home, that he was to vanish completely. Nor did she know that Aliyah's mother had no idea where the father had taken their daughter, or why he had suddenly vanished.

Aliyah felt lost between the elderly servant and the mistress as she watched her father, until, like lightening, he was gone. Touching her forehead at the spot where her father had kissed her – that one, orphan kiss – it felt as though a star shone through her fingers. Aliyah was happy. The kiss brought a fleeting glimmer to her eyes, which caught the mistress's attention as she approached.

Tossed amongst the mirror's projections, the memory came back to Hanan of that first glow she had noticed in Aliyah's eyes, at a moment in which she was still the mistress examining her new maid.

The yellow cloth wrapping Aliyah's head was the second thing to attract her. Hanan approached, trying to work out what it was exactly that her servant had placed over her hair. The faded red lines looked like traces of blood, but as she got closer, she saw that they were the remnants of old threads. Hanan smelt a penetrating scent: the mother's laundry. She stood there and stroked her fingers across the little girl's head. She bent down, then squatted as she peered into the girl's dark eyes. Intent on discovering where she was and what was expected of her, she stared straight back; her heart pounded, but her gaze was undisturbed by the slightest blink. The mistress explored the little girl's features; they were too finely sculpted, too beautiful for a servant. Hanan brimmed with happiness at the discovery. Most maids had a generic expression, somewhere between doltish sadness and patient sorrow. Their cheeks, thought Hanan, were not pronounced like Aliyah's; most were red and puffy, like the cooks' faces, or pale and sagging, like the housemaids'. Aliyah's face was like that of a black panther; were it not for the fear and sadness that sometimes appeared in the girl's expression then Hanan al-Hashimi would have been afraid as she circled the little girl, examining her from head to toe.

Hanan reached out a hand towards Aliyah's head and pulled off the cloth. She did not unfasten the flower clip, which scratched the girl's cheek. Her coarse hair was revealed, pulled back in a short, tight plait, so small it was barely noticeable. Where the flower clip had been there was now a brilliant red line, from which sprung a drop of crimson blood. Aliyah stayed glued to the spot in silence. She realised it was her duty to please the mistress, who had paid her family a lot of money. It was really very simple; all she had to do was obey.

Aliyah thought of nothing else but to fulfil her mistress's wishes. That way, her mother would no longer have to work in other people's houses and her brothers and sisters would get to buy nice clothes, she thought. She was only there for them. With that in mind, everything was easy. She didn't raise her hand to try to see the hot liquid, even though she could feel its sting on her cheek. There wasn't the slightest crease of emotion in her expression. Aliyah blinked slightly when the mistress leant towards her to wipe away the blood with her embroidered handkerchief.

'I didn't mean to,' said the mistress hoarsely as she dabbed Aliyah's face, cleansing the shallow wound, which had left a clear mark on her cheek.

'I really didn't mean to.' Hanan was addressing herself, reproachfully. She waited for a response, but the little girl didn't make a sound; she simply grabbed hold of her head-covering and attempted to put it back in its place.

'It won't do you any harm to take it off inside the house.'

Aliyah peered at the mistress in bewilderment. She wasn't used to baring her head to strangers – she could burn in hell for such a thing. Even the mistress wore a hijab; hers was delicately embroidered. She made no response, instead simply lowering her hand, the hijab too, and nodding her agreement. The mistress pulled away the cloth and threw it aside. As she grabbed hold of her hand, she was momentarily taken aback by the warmth of the little girl's palm.

'Come, I'll show you to your room. We'll be staying here a few more days then you'll get a much nicer one,' she said, thinking of the colourful room in the villa which she had prepared for guests. Hanan could barely believe her own actions: how could she be giving away the guestroom just like that? When had she made that decision? And how had the heat of the little girl's palm transferred like that to her own body? It must just be pity, she thought. After all, the girl was no more than a maid!

Hanan began to recall that first glimmer in the little girl's eyes and how she had grabbed hold of her hand. All that was left to her now, she thought, was the nightmare – the streak of light. If there wasn't a knock at the door soon, if her brown-skinned maid didn't enter, then she might live the rest of her days in a vacant state.

In that very same moment, Aliyah looked up at the closed window for the last time, standing up from the marble wall as she slipped the photograph into her bag and vanished with the wind.

The images ended their dance around Hanan al-Hashimi's room – the room of the closed window – and she became certain that the streak of light had not been a dream. Hanan thought about phoning Nazek, but it was still very early, and she might cause a scandal. Besides, what would she say to her? Yet, she did want Nazek with her right then. Hanan snatched her mobile. She dialled. No response. Cursing Nazek silently, she threw herself onto the bed, feeling death on her trail once more. Completely alone in her room, it was just like all those years ago when her family had taken the hasty decision that she would marry her cousin. She was just like the girl she had been back then, Hanan thought.

Twenty years had passed, perhaps more? In those days she had looked for excuses to stay in her room, or to go to the university – anything but to sit with her mother and the rest of the family. She fled those dreary discussions of her beauty, of how unlucky she was to be marrying a sterile man, how she would work hard to complete her studies after their marriage. On and on they went...

Hanan wished for death to visit the house and take somebody away. Death was the only thing capable of making life less miserable. If her husband were to pass away, she would truly be indebted to God. But it wasn't to be. Instead, her father died and, after holding out for many long years, her mother too passed away one winter. Aliyah was the only person whose departure from the world Hanan never imagined, and now she had passed on.

Hanan al-Hashimi cried out. Looking towards the window, she contemplated getting up to pull back the curtains, but decided to remain still. She was dead now! The idea calmed her.

As she lay corpse-like on her bed, Hanan's body was as it had always been, like that of a nubile boy: a slight chest, slim waist, the buttocks of a ten-year old, without the least trace of a curve to them, and slender lips. Once, her husband had tried to kiss her and she had screamed in pain. After that, Hanan had stayed in her room for days, ashamed of her own lips. Later, she told her mother that her husband had wanted to swallow her up beginning with her lips.

Hanan would tell her mother the most intimate details of what went on in her husband's bedroom. If she did not, her mother would find out somehow. She regretted never having instructed her daughter in the bedroom arts, as *Shami* women normally did, for their girls to keep hold of their husbands and lure them into night-time's pleasures. But by the time Hanan's mother came to teach her the arts, the moment had already passed. Any new instruction made her all the more shy and frigid. Could she really drag her husband into bed? How? Hanan would burn with hatred as she stood before her mother. Why must she stay there being told what to do? To want it, not to hold back; to hold back, not to refuse; to flirt with him until he burns with desire; to tease him with his own servitude and make him feel like the crown on her head; to massage his feet and sprinkle his body with the oil her mother had brought her from the perfume market, then to feed him, morsel by morsel, though not always. It was a question of push and pull, a precarious balancing act. Both coquetry and prudence were required at the same time. A few moments were sufficient to make his heart pound, and a man's heart is found between two regions: the thighs, the zone where the blood pumps from before spreading to the rest of the man's body, her mother said. Hanan began to giggle uncontrollably, quite convinced that her mother had no understanding of science at all. Blood is pumped from the heart, she informed her mother, who turned to her daughter and muttered, 'Silly girl... down below is where the stallion's tethered, you little know-it-all!'

Hanan's mother would continue talking until her daughter

had fallen asleep. Then she would leave the room in defeat, giving up on the simple-minded girl who was not a bit like her mother.

'Stupid girl, nothing like her mother.' On those words, Hanan closed her eyes.

Hanan waved her hands in front of her face, as though shaking away the dust. She jumped to her feet once more and opened the window, looking out at the horizon which seemed clearer with the approaching dawn. The faint outline of a slow-moving figure was just noticeable – a black speck of a creature.

'Is that Aliyah?'

At the sound of her own voice, Hanan returned to the mirror, wanting to discover just how delirious she had become.

～

She walked slowly, not only because of the bag which weighed her down, but because that way, she might keep moving without coming to any destination. Aliyah was afraid that her family would have disappeared and she would have to confront fate itself.

Why hadn't she heard any news from them in all those years? What could possibly have happened? Out of nowhere, a terrible thought seized her: what if a fire had broken out and taken them all? Then, just as quickly, she felt euphoric, seduced by the hope that perhaps her father alone had met his death and neither her mother nor her brothers and sisters had known the way to Hanan and Anwar's villa. But the joy was destroyed as swiftly as it had arisen; it was impossible that death could have even come close to that tyrant. Perhaps he had disappeared with a woman and the way to the villa was not known, since it was the old house that he had taken her to, where he had counted the bundle of notes twice, and then left.

Her walk towards home brought back the feelings of that day – the day of the picture, which was stored safely in her bag.

After her fight with the boys, he was waiting for her at home. In the rain she had walked slowly – just like now – as though to delay confrontation. But time marched on and the way to the room was short. There was no escape; she had come to the place where she slept at night and there was nothing to do but enter.

When Aliyah arrived at the door to their room she found it banging against the frame and was surprised that her mother had left it so, allowing their body heat to escape. She did not know that those were the orders her father had given, as he lay in his usual position stretched out on his mat, exhaling the smoke of his cheap cigarette and waiting in fury for his devil of a daughter to arrive. He wore nothing but a thin shirt and a pair of coal-coloured jeans. It was around that time that he had adopted the habit of twirling his moustache pensively, before picking up a small mirror and gazing into it. 'My youth all gone, wasted and lost,' he would mutter. Then he would curse his wife, the woman who had embroiled him in a life of difficulties the moment he had married her.

What would he look like now, she wondered. Had he changed much? Would he recognise her? What would she say to him? That her mistress had thrown her out? Why had she thrown her out?

Aliyah's father was a dark, strangely attractive man. His skin was a golden, coffee colour and his voice deep and gruff. All of the women in the neighbourhood envied his wife, even more so after one unfortunate night when he had come out of the house and displayed his equipment for all of them to see. 'It's so big, it needs four women!' they teased Aliyah's mother after that.

The women would turn green with envy as they watched Aliyah's mother stagger towards them in the mornings while gathering around the bus, to set out for the homes all over Damascus where they worked. Aliyah's mother never paid their comments any attention. Fate had caught her in a trap between pleasing her husband, who spent most of the time unemployed, fulfilling her employers' wishes, and taking care of her nightmare children, who would have her running after them in the middle of the night to drag them from the streets.

Even though she had worked in other people's houses since she had married him, when she had first realised that there would be no peace with this man and no money from him, she still retained an inkling of pride in being his wife. Yes, he plucked his pubic hair with the tweezers she used for her eyebrows, and yes, he insisted on having sex several times a day. 'He is never satisfied!' she would tell the women of the neighbourhood. Her complaints were genuine, yet tempered with pride.

He would wake her up in the middle of the night, when her strength was spent from the day's work, and pull her out of bed, anxious not to wake the children. In the beginning, he would screw her just next to the bed, but then his daughters – Aliyah the biggest gossip of them all – began telling the neighbourhood women about what their father got up to at night. After that he became more cautious, dragging his semi-conscious wife into the bathroom – the space which doubled as a kitchen and was barely wide enough for two to stand. He would make her kneel, then mount her for a few minutes, before withdrawing quickly. At first, Aliyah's mother would cry, but once she got used to his behaviour and her movements became automatic, he no longer had to ask. She would take off her clothes and lay still beneath him and when he had finished, she would wash quickly, without looking him in the face. Afterwards she would return hastily to bed where she plunged into a deep sleep.

In the morning, she would gesture that her back was hurting, in the hope of just a single day's peace. 'A woman who doesn't follow her husband's orders in bed doesn't go to heaven,' he would say, without meeting her eyes. Aliyah's mother shook her head. 'And where's the bed?' As he fell silent, she grew a little more courageous and raised her voice. 'I can't, not every day. My back's killing me from working all the daylight hours.' But he avoided meeting her eyes and when evening came, he would do just the same as the previous night, telling her that if he didn't have sex with her every day, he would find a prostitute instead. The threat always made Aliyah's mother cry, not because she was jealous, but because she feared that he would take the money needed for the children's food and spend it on a prostitute. She kept quiet, then went out to work, while he stayed at home with the children, who would do all they could to please their father. Even though it was she who did the house work and put bread on the table, she left it to him to give orders, as a man and the true master of the household. And so, when he asked her to leave the door open, she didn't say a word, sensing the extent of his rage. She decided not to interfere in his manner of punishing his daughter. After all, he was the man of the house and the girl's father, and a girl had to learn to face her elders, or so she repeatedly told herself. She didn't want him to leave, not because she loved him – whatever love there was had departed in the early days – but because she lived life by the words her mother had taught her: 'Any man's better than no man at all.'

Aliyah stumbled along the dusty track, struggling to drag her bag. She tried to see through the curtains covering Hanan al-Hashimi's closed window.

'Any man's better than no man at all,' she called out sarcastically. Aliyah listened to her mother's words as they fell into the air and her anger intensified, her mind returning to al-Raml.

On entering the house, she had found the door open and her father still stretched out on the floor. Her clothes were in tatters. She licked away her snot and dried the tears from her face, which was stained with streaks of chocolate. Now that she had stopped moving, her body had started to turn blue with cold and her breathing was loud and rasping. Tears came and she gasped for air as if teetering on the edge of an abyss. Aliyah stared at her mother, who forced herself to appear not to care; were she to take her daughter in her arms as she wanted to, she knew that the girl's father would fly into a rage. He didn't wait long before grabbing Aliyah by the hair and pulling her into the room, where he started to kick her, screaming death to her whore of a mother for bearing him daughters. Her mother began to plead with him to let the girl be, biting her lip hard each time he called her the daughter of a whore. 'But I'm the one who puts food on the table,' she muttered repeatedly, her voice barely audible.

Aliyah had never known her father to lose it like that. She couldn't understand what provoked him to want to kill his own children. The thought of the first punch, or the first strike of his giant foot against her body filled her with terror, but she soon lost consciousness, only to wake up a few hours later with every limb of her body in pain. Her mother's refusal to go to work so she could look after her daughter – her way of punishing him for the beating – exacerbated his frustration. She wept all day as he cursed and swore, having realised that his wife would not be returning with the necessary provisions to fill the hungry stomachs surrounding him.

It was the same image of him which seemed to be coming towards her now, drawing closer from the distant horizon as she stumbled along on her high-heels. Aliyah paused for a minute and turned her head. The window was still closed and from a distance it seemed a dark, black speck.

She had no other hope but to return to al-Raml. The district formed a partial wall around Damascus, like a viper encircling the city. On the inside of the wall, the city was cramped, standing motionless before the parade of concrete houses and the peculiar clans of people setting out in every direction, in search of a morsel of bread.

Despite the sectarianism which, over recent decades, had given each clan its own character – from al-Riz district, to 'Ash al-Wurud, to Jaramana Camp – each group resembled the rest and they were all interconnected. Their slums reached out into the heart of the city, like Dwel'a, which stretched into Jaramana and on to Bab Touma.

Al-Raml was home to an odd assortment of poor folk, who had carried their humiliating poverty with them when they fled to south Damascus. The people built small rooms for themselves from sheets of tin and badly made cement bricks. Impoverished Palestinians and dark-skinned Ghouranis – people of the Jordan Valley – lived alongside the destitute people who had arrived one day from the coastal mountains, dividing into large groups. The new arrivals lived in miserable settlements, established chaotically by mobsters, cheats and traffickers. Senior military officers took hold of the fringes of the city and sent their own 'communities' to live there, the new settlements forming the officers' spheres of influence. They created 'ghettos' too, laid out like a monochrome mosaic, the colour of poverty and despair. Those who migrated from the neighbouring countryside and from more distant rural areas, dreaming of a decent life, became mercenaries, bodyguards, secret police and smugglers. The rest – among them the people of al-Raml – turned their daughters into servants, just as they had done over a hundred years previously when the girls were pawned to Aleppan tradesmen. Meanwhile, the girls' fathers became day labourers, scattered about Damascus's public squares, where they would accept any offer of work that came their way. Very quickly, the district attracted a group of poor university students, who lived by the dozens in adjoining rooms. Tenth-rate prostitutes settled in the area too, making deals with the taxi drivers to bring in the night-time punters. The place was an oddity, even to itself. There wasn't the slightest sense of closeness drawing the neighbours together, or linking the adjoining houses, even though the residents could hear their neighbours' lustful cries at night. In the mornings, the women would joke about the noises they heard, imitating the animal cries as they crowded in the doorways, before most left for work.

Al-Raml district was like a public square that was alien to its own times. Everything there seemed comical, like a cartoon or a black-and-white western. The place was arid, isolated and languishing in dust: the glass windows covered with cardboard;

the rusty iron doors; the walls made of tin and iron sheeting; the little shops like bandits' grottos; the houses on top of houses. This latter sort was rare, perhaps because of the innovative way in which they were constructed. The owners would fix four iron posts into the ground, cover the walls with pieces of durable sheet iron and then hold them together with a little cement. Were it not for the rattling winter gales, this would have provided protection against the wind and made the walls solid. The roof was fixed with the same sort of resistant iron sheeting, held in place with a few kilograms of cement. There wouldn't necessarily be a window to the room; the gaps in the walls, which appeared in every building despite the precautions taken, provided ventilation. On a winter's day those very same holes became streams of rainwater.

The other innovative way to create a home with adjoining rooms was to construct a partitioning wall which acted as two, since it was attached to two rooms. Then, both rooms would be covered with tin sheeting and the inner sides of the stone walls masked with pieces of coloured fabric, stuck down with cement until they became a part of the wall. After that, all the residents had to do was spread a mat on the floor and gather a few covers, and the place would become a real paradise.

It was striking how the men's eyes in al-Raml drowned in fatigue, despite the women's beautiful faces, made up with bright red lipstick as they strolled by, flirting restlessly. This strange neighbourhood – cloaked in dust and boredom – was capable of turning even the red shades of the women's lips a sombre, ashen tone, since deep down the men realised that the girls' flirting glances were put on for the first pleasure-seeker they came across.

The alleyways which ran between these buildings acted as a

sort of boundary, no more than half a metre wide, which kept the women inside as their bellies swelled year upon year. During the final months of their pregnancy, the women were prevented from leaving the house, since their inflated stomachs couldn't possibly fit through the tight alleyways all at once. The fact that there was a mosque in the neighbourhood made al-Raml all the more peculiar. Its magnificence was an oddity amongst the startling gloom of the houses. The mosque was built from iron and cement and decorated with marble. It was constructed by a charity worker, to provide a space for the neighbourhood men to gather in the evenings and sort out their differences and to receive handouts from the charities. The mosque's Imam came from al-Midan and was not a local, but over the previous few years he had become a guardian to the whole community. Even though he was over fifty and already had two wives, the Imam married a third time – a girl from al-Raml who could have been no older than fifteen. He had spotted her one day as he made his way back from the mosque and she was leaving the house with her head uncovered, he felt a shiver run straight through his body as he leered at her curvaceous backside.

The people of al-Raml could still recollect how everything had changed after the man from the religious charity had built them a mosque, and how the women started to behave differently. When the man began bringing groups of his followers there, with their long beards and loose trousers, most of the women began to cover their heads. The man would bless them during his Friday sermons and beseech the other women to join them in rejecting sin.

Aliyah's father visited the mosque daily. He found solace in the courtyard and his visits gave him the opportunity to catch up on the neighbourhood gossip, but the other men would avoid him, fearing his volatile temper. Even though they freely allowed their wives to work for unmarried men, the women were warned against Aliyah's father nonetheless. The men envied him for his beautiful Ghourani wife, who was tall and wonderfully full-figured with dark eyes, slender lips and a bronze glow to her hair. Hearing her screams in the daytime when he hit her for some trivial reason, or in the evening when he took her by force, the men were of one opinion – that Aliyah's father was unworthy of his wife.

A cold sweat, born of fear, seeped through Aliyah's clothes, heightening her sensitivity to the morning chill as the gust of a passing lorry swept over her. Something about the lorry reminded her of her father. Perhaps it was the dust storm that had almost knocked her off her feet, just like her father's tempests, which left no opposition standing.

Aliyah stood fixed to the spot as she remembered the night when her mother had gone out into the alleyway, wailing and having torn her clothing in grief. The events of that night were crystal clear in her memory; she could still hear her elder sister's voice.

Her sister had been on her way back from work in one of the factories, where they made socks, not far from al-Raml. Many such places, around the suburbs of Damascus were described as factories in exaggeration; in actuality, they were workshops running on the energy of young women working for little pay, who were happy to complete the tasks their bosses gave them without insurance since, after all, it was better to work morning and night than to loiter on the streets of Damascus in search of a late-night punter.

Aliyah Senior was one of those young women. She was given an opportunity that many girls were not, after having almost mastered the craft. Life had been hard for her, accompanying her mother from one house to another, assisting with the cleaning, carrying heavy goods for the dainty mistresses, preparing teas and coffees and tidying the textiles workshop. Eventually, she became a skilled seamstress herself and took up her position behind a machine. Aliyah Senior worked earnestly in everything she did. It was important to please her boss, she felt, her mind focused solely on helping her mother to provide some stability for the family. Aliyah would daydream that her father might unexpectedly meet his death. It would be a relief if he went, she thought, not only because he took hold of the whole household income, but because without him her mother's annual pregnancies would cease and life's burdens would no longer grow. She rarely thought about buying herself a new dress, nor did she expect to receive any attention from the boys as she followed her daily route, crossing the threshold of the family's room and walking until she reached the workshop door.

Her calmness and nonchalance made Aliyah a dream girl to the boys who loitered in the alleyways, and yet it was the factory boss whom she let fondle her, although within certain limits. Aliyah would restrict his advances, particularly when he reached his hand between her thighs. He could pull down his trousers and she would allow him to kiss her breasts, but never to approach the danger zone – that deep part of her anatomy which, if trespassed, would bring shame on her family. Aliyah had the feeling that she was courting danger, that there was a dividing line between keeping him at bay and holding on to her job.

As she washed her face clean of the boss's slaver, Aliyah

thought about arrangements for the coming month and slipped the money into her pocket. Prudently, she kept a small amount back, without the slightest suspicion of what was to happen on her return home. She was still wearing her work dress, her socks and headscarf when her father appeared out of nowhere. Aliyah jumped. They had been busy, she and her pregnant mother, counting the costs of a numerous family. Perhaps it was her mother's bad luck which had prompted him to enter at the very moment she had spread the notes out on the thin sponge mattress. No, her mother wasn't the bad omen: it was her.

On that ill-fated evening, he came in calmly and silently, watching his wife and daughter as they muttered away whilst counting the money. He was a tall man, with an inclining frame, which often leant him a romantic quality and had caused his wife to fall in love at first sight. The slight curve of his posture wasn't his only attractive quality; smooth black hair, a full moustache, a deep voice and piercing stare all contributed to the man's appeal. Little Aliyah had inherited that stare, with all of its harshness, its power and weakness. Her father was aware of his own authority over his wife; he knew that she was in love with him, that he would be obeyed as he wished to be, and that the mother had passed on this sense of obedience to her daughters. The father was content with his life of ease, he told himself, although he said the opposite to his family. But when he entered the room and saw the bank notes spread out on the sponge mattress, he felt as though things were slipping beyond his control. He would teach his women a lesson they would never forget, so he told himself. Humming, he pushed the door open and confronted his wife immediately, who felt terror spread through her limbs. Meanwhile, Aliyah Senior quickly gathered up the money and concealed it in her apron, knowing that he would seize everything she had at the end of the month and disappear for a few days, only to return empty-handed, telling them that policemen on patrol had seized all the contraband cigarettes he had bought, and that he hadn't managed to sell a single carton.

Aliyah Senior was scared. She bit down on her tongue. The syllables stumbled from her blue lips as she tried to keep hold of the money, her hands clasped like claws around weakened prey.

As Aliyah buried her face in her mother's lap, her mother was thinking of how to protect her own swollen middle. She had finally got used to being beaten, but this time the father's rage had come unexpectedly. He pounced on Aliyah and grabbed her by the hair, which became a rope in his hands that he wrapped around his fingers. He swung the girl's body against the walls, which shook as the money poured out of her apron and onto the ground. The mother screamed, her stomach quivering before her. He hit her and she fled from the room, her hair uncovered. In full view of the neighbours, Aliyah's mother began to rip her clothes, wailing and screaming for the men to save her daughter, who had fallen unconscious. Some of the men from the alley entered the room and grabbed hold of her husband, who pushed them away violently. Pursuing them to the doorway, he pulled down his trousers and thrusted his genitalia in front them.

'If any of you sons of bitches come any closer, I'll make you eat… this!' he shouted.

The men stared, not believing what they were seeing. Then, in dumbfoundment they retreated, while the women gawped at him, perplexed, before hurrying after their husbands.

Had the families' expressions been less hateful and disapproving, he would probably have gone back into the room. Instead, he stood shaking with anger, before returning to gather the money and vanishing. With no knowledge that his wife had bled until she had lost the baby, he spent three days wandering the streets. The thought that his eldest daughter would pass the short remainder of her life bedridden didn't even enter his mind. From then on, her mother would wash her and wrap her with towels around her pelvis, just as she had done when she was little. She would wipe away the excrement and urine and pray to God that she would wake up in the morning and find that the Almighty had answered her call; that He had taken her daughter's soul and released her from her torment.

A year after the incident which left her sister crippled, Aliyah was born. She was given another name, which her mother forgot after Aliyah Senior's death when, as a good omen, she took to calling the younger girl by the name of her dead sister, overwhelming her with a level of care that not one of her five children – whom sickness would soon reduce to three – enjoyed.

Aliyah set out on her way again, far from Hanan al-Hashimi. She would take on her big sister's role as her mother's helper, she had decided. She cursed the mistress, spitting with every step. The weight of the bag – or the memories – was too heavy to bear. Aliyah sat down and dried herself of the cold sweat, wondering how long it would be until she found sleep like her sister had. When would her father's next fit of fury come? When would she meet her death?

Aliyah with her bag: the black speck which Hanan al-Hashimi spotted from the gap in the curtains covering the tightly shut window. She started to walk again, slowly and laboriously, or so Hanan imagined as she retreated from the window, gasping for air between sobs. The girl's hesitance wasn't a sign that she was waiting for Hanan to call her to come back; it only showed her reluctance to head in the only direction there was. For Aliyah there was only one destination: al-Raml.

~

The little one realised she had awoken from the dream and there was no way to get it back. Hanan too had lost a lot to forces beyond her control and now she was alone in her wide bed, biting her nails in regret over that moment when she had expelled her maid.

Who was Aliyah? Hanan wondered. Her servant? Really? *Who is she?* Aliyah was the mistress of the house and Hanan knew it, but at what point their roles had reversed, she couldn't recall. When had Aliyah proceeded forward with her princess-like majesty to claim the throne? And when was it that Hanan seized it back from her, turning her back into nothing but a skinny, char-skinned girl?

In the beginning, Hanan had attempted to act particularly tough in front of the petrified maid as she helped her to arrange her belongings and showed her how to act properly. Back then she would spend most of her days out of the house, not thinking to return except to sleep. How had Aliyah made her prisoner to this room?

After her mother's death, Hanan had lived without family. Her uncles had moved to the ends of the earth, scattering over North and Latin America and taking the entirety of the family's riches with them. Out of all of the family members, two brothers had remained. They owned a few shops in al-Bazouriyeh, a stall selling cotton garments in Souq al-Hamidiyeh and several houses in 'Ain al-Kirsh in al-Salihiyyeh district. Their collection of businesses grew gradually, until the brothers became two of the biggest businessmen in Damascus. The elder of the two had one son and a wife who had already passed away, while the other had just one daughter whom he raised as though she were the family's only son. Because of the love he had felt for his wife, the elder brother never remarried; a decision that the cold-hearted members of his family could not come to understand, having never much approved of their scion's affection for his wife.

When she was still small, Hanan would hear her uncle tell everyone that his brother's wife was the boss of him, day and night, in the bed and out of it. At the time, Hanan felt nothing against her uncle, since her tough old mother, who never took her in her arms, had a unique ability to attract disapproval from everyone around her, and particularly from Hanan, who wished she'd been born a boy. Hanan's mother went to great lengths to ignore her maternal instincts, believing it would make an exceptional person of her daughter, and allow her to be proud of the way she had raised her. Hanan would be her compensation for not having a son to carry on the family name. Not wishing to spoil her family's idea of her, Hanan was a calm and obedient child. Her ability to remain pacified accompanied her throughout life and, for a long time, she succeeded in giving her small family the impression that she was at peace. When she started to accompany her cousin to his parties, she would appear constantly startled by what she saw, wary of everything. She tried to avoid attracting the others' attention, imagining that each of them was ready and waiting to criticise or disparage her. She continued repeating her mother's words in her head. When her family praised her, looking at her with great affection and boasting secretly amongst themselves of how well-mannered and serene she was, she felt ready to scream so hard that her heart would explode, right in her mother's face. But she never quite dared.

Everything in Hanan's world was unbearably regimented, programmed to move on a straight course without a chance for detour. In her lowest moments, Hanan didn't dare to scream how she felt before her family; such behaviour was shameful and she would only be forced to apologise later on. Her punishment would be a lengthy ban from sitting with the family. She would be locked in her bedroom with the curtains drawn, whilst the others were banned from spending any significant amount of time talking to her. They would punish her with silence and loneliness and she would feel she was on the cusp of going mad. Hanan would have preferred to be punished like the neighbours' daughters were – with beatings – but for the al-Hashimi family, such behaviour was uncivilised. Even her cousin would suspend communication with her, following suit with the others.

After her marriage, the only way Hanan knew how to keep within the limits laid down for her was to become more sub-servient to others and steer further away from any internal reflection. She never complained of the degradation she suffered while living with her cousin – how at night, she felt as though she were about to suffocate under his weight, until he stood up from her and went to the bathroom. He would come back mumbling lines of the Qur'an, praying to God to bring him a son to be an heir for his family once he was gone. Perhaps if Hanan had paid a little attention to the impulsive, lust-driven movements which sometimes took control of her husband, then she would have found some happiness. But she felt not the slightest bit interested. The thought of him betraying her with another woman gave her none of a wife's anxiety.

And he had no need for her worry anyway; he would ask the Lord for forgiveness for his fantasies. Yet God-fearing though he was, Anwar al-Hashimi was not deterred from entering into business deals so great they would transform Hanan's world completely and leave him feeling disgruntled at having to register his possessions and his money under both of their names. He would watch Hanan with a combination of pleasure and contempt, as though she were still the little girl he had once known, as though she had never grown up.

Opening her eyes, Hanan began to caress her middle, just above her barren womb, which had never produced a family heir. Only a few hours earlier, Aliyah's fingers had roamed that same area, her lips too. As she lay on the bed, Hanan brought back to mind her memories of Aliyah, attempting to understand who the girl was exactly and who she was herself. As the scent of cinnamon wafted over her once more, she was submerged in a new wave of sadness. She shut her eyes and wound her arms around her chest. Peering out of the window, Hanan spotted Aliyah – a black dot getting smaller and smaller. In that moment, Anwar's image appeared before her, just as he was on her first night. Hanan's heart skipped a beat and her skin crawled at the sight of Aliyah's fingers wrapped around Anwar's dangling penis. Sharp contractions shot through her abdomen and she ran to the bathroom, where she vomited until her stomach was empty. Lying on the bathroom floor, Hanan sensed the coolness of the porcelain tiles and felt a little calmer.

Moment by moment, Hanan examined each of her feelings

as they arose, catching herself in the act. Her longing for Aliyah consumed her completely; she still couldn't quite believe the girl was truly gone. On the floor, Hanan studied her fingers. They were so ugly, she thought, so wrinkled and ugly now. Recalling the touch of Aliyah's fingers against her cheek, her stomach started to contract once more.

Aliyah had played with her here on this same cold floor. Hanan could hear the girl's voice floating over the foamy bath-water whilst her eyes followed what she said curiously:

'You know, I've never felt anything sweeter than the pleasure your fingers give me. There's nothing that burns like your desire does… That's what leads its fingers to the hiding places of your pain – the pain running through your blood, beneath your skin. When you reach a climax that makes you feel as though you're suffocating suddenly Allah will provide you an opening from yourself. No, it will never come like this! You must mould it from your own clay, you alone.

'I turn into a crescent moon; I become a secret. Everything must be kept in secrecy; it's our only life-line here.

'Don't provoke others with the way you look at them. Smile and speak sweetly. You have to be happy with life, and happiness is to become a sealed glass snow globe, full of falling snowflakes – however others shake you, they can't work out what's inside. That is power: to be both origin and ending within yourself. Nobody will dare to even come close to you then. Step-by-step, you begin to bathe with your own soul; your fingers are your captain and your mind is the source of your senses; the place where your tremors are born.'

Hanan looked away from her fingers, caressing her body as she whispered to herself almost silently:

'No man can give you pleasure like supple fingers can; their touch comes from your heart and not from a man's body. Warm protrusions, opening up inside you, expanding, granting all that originated from you and all that is within you. By that you are mistress of your own self. In a shudder, your womanliness returns to you and you remain erect. Fingers are like *alifs* that resonate forever. They arise from the void and soar through the air and, as their trembling touch fondles the abyss, they generate an eternal bliss, which begins and ends in the same moment. There are all sorts of delicious fingers. Yours are slender and rough, but beautiful. Do you know mine? Sometimes they seize up – they freeze in the middle of things and then won't follow through, not knowing how to move. They finish when my love of them is just beginning. Have you ever made love with your fingers? Fingers don't end in humiliating flaccidity. Any time you ask them to, they'll come to you. Mine love to roam your body. They don't like my lips, or my eyes. I hate my fingers! They have the power to harm me whenever they get away. My fingers are made of sand. Don't look at how white they are. They're full of air, so with their very first touch they melt away. So soft. Your fingers are firm – nothing like a limp piece of crocodile flesh. When you grow up you'll experience it for yourself. How can you stay so defenceless to the storm of pleasure? You haven't yet tested this for yourself, you haven't felt yourself overflow and the flame die out before you sense that deep inside boiling up. Do you know what crocodiles are like? They have thick, dangling penises and their smell is like death. Have you seen the face of my old crocodile? You've seen him? But you haven't smelt him. That smell, it's not old age. He's always smelt like that. Then and now. Do you know what it's like to lie beneath an old crocodile – a foaming, drooling, panting crocodile? I had to do it all the time… I would be lying beneath his flesh, in this terrifying place where there's nothing but shadow – between the crocodile's skin and the sound of his breathing. That was before I discovered my own fingers, growing in the crocodile's pool, before they led me to climax and I stripped away my lizard's skin – I was a lizard, used to a man who never cried. Crocodiles don't cry; their eyes are forever glazed. Do you know, he never cried. Not once. He has that smell of the dead about him – the smell of beings who feed upon your lifeblood and then, at dawn, withdraw in defeat to their beds. His bed covers were made of velvet. Can you believe it? Coffins are lined with velvet. Red velvet. Smooth fabric doesn't suit the brittleness of death. Why can't they line coffins with cotton instead? I adore your fingers – look how upright they appear! You don't know your fingers, and they don't know you either – but I know them. I adore them and I adore the way your skin feels. I certainly don't love my crocodile's scales. Do crocodiles have scales, or are they little needles concealed between the folds of the skin? Will you play with me a little? Look, the water's warm. It's… colourless. White, or the colour of the bath tub, white and hot? You're so beautiful. Your fingers are so long and… When you were little did you ever try to take refuge from your loneliness in your fingers? Nobody ever understood me. I would look to my fingers for shelter, in a house full of gloomy spirits and wide windows, inhabited by everything but life. You've never learnt to speak your body's language – I'll teach you. You're still a child; you haven't yet discovered your secret power source. If you had, you would have grown up faster. Are you going to stay a child for much longer? When will you grow up? Little mute. Are you mute? Do you not know how to speak? That's the worst thing about you, and the most beautiful thing too. You will be a part of me. No, you can't be – you're a being of flesh and your eyes are so sly. Never mind, I'll make you a part of… well, maybe even… Perhaps you can sit in front of me on the comodino, like a mannequin. You don't look much like a mannequin. What do you look like? I'm not sure. You're so delicate and soft and obedient, like a cat. No, you're not soft – not yet. But you will be.'

Aliyah was afraid of Hanan. She felt alarmed as Hanan calmly investigated her body. Hanan's fingers played over the little body, moving them over her eyes like a pianist. She twisted the girl's hands and looked lustfully at her fingers. The little girl didn't understand much of what her mistress was saying; she was completely overwhelmed upon finding herself in this magic realm. Aliyah never concentrated much during those long sessions in the bathroom, as she spread oil and foamy soap over her mistress's body, in accordance with her instructions. The most beguiling thing was the ornate copper tea pot, which boiled continuously, on top of a peculiar basin. Later, she discovered that the pot was heated electrically, keeping the tea warm quietly and consistently. Hanan would steady the pot on a marble ledge next to the bath tub, then fill it with cinnamon sticks. She would let the steam fill the air around her, breathing in and out in controlled breaths. When the water in the kettle had evaporated completely, she would refill it. Every time she started a new pot, she would place a transparent, gold-rimmed glass next to it; a glass unlike anything Aliyah had ever seen before. It was very rare, Hanan told her; it had been her great grandfather's and she had drunk her tea from it since she was ten years old. Hanan recalled the little girl's joy in sipping tea with her from the special glass. She struck her hand painfully against the porcelain floor, screaming:

'She's not coming back!'

~

'I'm not going back!'

Aliyah hit the heels of her shoes against the ground as she cursed Hanan using foul expressions. She imagined jumping on her from behind and slicing her with her knife, just as she had once done to the neighbourhood boys. 'Fucking bitch… Fucking bitch,' she heard her own voice croak, muttering the words into space.

Opening her eyes, Aliyah stared into the horizon stretched out before her. The compact mansions were silent. The scent of the desert had a reinvigorating effect, but her bag was still heavy and her body had started to wane with fatigue. It had not been an ordinary night: the mistress and the master, the streak of light, ghosts of al-Raml and, to top it all off, there before her was her elder sister, carrying her along on her magic carpet, encouraging her to keep going.

She felt a prickling sensation around her neck and remembered the gold chain, reaching out her hand to feel it. The necklace was a gift from Hanan. She could sell it, she thought – a reassuring idea. Then she would be able to take some things back for her brothers and sisters, and her mother too. After all, it wouldn't be right to return after so many years without even a few sweets or some fruit. The tin-sheet room occupied Aliyah's mind. Imaginings of her future in al-Raml took over her thoughts. But the visions were not alone; for a little while now another image – that of a closed window – had gnawed away at her mind.

Aliyah remembered how she and her siblings would trample on each other's toes as they gathered full circle around a large aluminium dish on the floor, placed in the exact centre of the room. It was difficult to tell precisely whose fingers were reaching towards the bowl; hands scrambled chaotically, rising from the dish, before they delved into mouths so cavernous it seemed they would never get out. Huddled together, the children would push and shove. Sometimes they joked with each other, but usually they swore and hurled insults, while their mother watched over them from a corner of the room, keeping an eye out for any sign of one of her children attempting to push another. After the youngest brother was once pushed head-first into the bowl, the mother had grown cautious to avoid a repeat incident. The boy's face had been covered with food and the rest of the dish had spilled onto the plastic mat, depriving the children of their dinner.

When the time came to sleep, the siblings would lie close together in special formation, each huddling on the floor with their arms tucked in to leave enough space for another member of the family. In winter especially, Aliyah felt herself slotted snuggly between the others like spoons in a drawer. In summer things were different; the bitter cold turned to blazing heat and the sheets of tin making up the roof and walls roasted their flesh. To sleep, the family would spread themselves across the plastic mat on the floor, since in summer the sponge mattress burnt their backs and the insects living inside became an instrument of torture, with their incessant scurrying and constant drone. The noise of the bugs and the biting mosquitoes buzzing about their ears kept everybody from sleeping.

Next to the sleep-stealing mosquitoes, everything else seemed insignificant. By the morning, the children's faces would have become swollen red lumps, which they scratched at, night and day, until the lumps bled and turned into little brown pimples. As a preventative measure, their mother would smack their scratching fingers. But there was something about the situation that the children didn't understand – something which made them lose control and attack their own skinny bodies. They would flee the house to the corners of the alleyways, where most of the other neighbourhood children came to scratch too, having escaped from their mothers. The children chose a corner far from view to hold their scratching parties and when they were finished, they returned home, their faces covered in blood and their eyes heavy with drowsiness. Aliyah was always afraid of leaving traces of blood on her face or on her legs; she knew that if her mother caught sight of the broken skin she would come at her with that strange, strong-smelling substance and dab it on the red patches. The ointment stung so strongly that she would kick out, jumping up and leaping about, until her mother pinned her to the floor and covered her body with the horrid ointment.

Aliyah tried to kick as she hobbled along on her high heels. 'I won't go back!' she insisted through gritted teeth.

She kicked the ground, then came to a halt. Swearing incomprehensibly, she lashed out at the pebbles on the side of the road, pummelling the stones like her father used to pummel her on those nights when one of his children started groaning or humming. The earth sent dust rising up around her, the whole place remaining deathly silent. She sneezed, then putting her bag down beside her, she continued to lash out at the ground. Surely the window would be open now, she thought. Aliyah recalled the faces of her brothers and sisters, frightened and packed in together at her side, with barely enough space to breathe. The children would stare, their eyes glistening bright like those of cats, terrified of the expressions they might transmit during their father's kicking sprees.

At night, Aliyah and her siblings would hide to escape their father's beatings, climbing under the woollen covers which their mother had woven from old jumpers. With the children's assistance, she spent the winter nights winding the thread of old garments into a ball, then re-weaving the wool into colourful patches. After completing several pieces, she would join the patches together with threads of thick wool, until the rug grew and became a warm blanket big enough to cover their bodies.

The family used the small inner room for cooking, washing and doing their business. There was a black pit to urinate in, framed by white cement. By the door they stacked the dishes on top of a stone basin, which they used for washing the crockery and pans. In the opposite corner was a large gas stove; every Thursday it was used to heat the bathing water. To the children, wash day was torture. Not only would they be shivering from the winter cold, but they would have to wait patiently in line for everybody else to finish washing. For the unfortunate child who was still bathing when the father decided he wanted a coffee, it was even worse. He wouldn't wait until they had finished pouring the small cups of water over their heads, but would kick the door open instead, barking at their mother to make him a coffee. Everybody froze still, their knees knocking together as they waited for the coffee pot to boil.

As the children grew up, there was no longer enough space for them to all bathe at once, and their mother extended wash day to a two-day event. After her lightening-speed wash, Aliyah would sit and roll between her fingers the short brown threads which peeled away from her skin when she rubbed it. It was Aliyah's great pleasure to see the threads of dirt and dead skin on her body. She would watch them with pride, feeling as though something had been made from her own body. Aliyah also showed her siblings how to form the little threads and keep them concealed within their palms. When the children's mother cottoned on to what they were doing, as the strings of dirt and dead skin mingled with the sweat in their clammy fists, Aliyah felt dismay. She would have to wait a whole other week before she could collect any new threads.

Aliyah was like a beast of prey and she delighted when others called her animal names. But sometimes, in her daydreams, she would notice peculiar things sprouting from her fingers, and a layer of hair covering her skin. Little black horns seemed to spring from her forehead and her teeth grew longer. Aliyah would scamper across the roofs of those packed-together rooms like a little wild animal.

That same sense of nimbleness returned to her as she heaved her bag and a faint happiness welled beneath her ribs at the return of her animal senses. She would leap about right there, she decided, just as she had done when she was small. She would frolic in the dirt, in the dawn twilight. The feeling that she was once again an animal made Aliyah feel protected from a fear of the unknown. Although she was alone, she was happy, and even though she didn't know where to turn to – heading back to her first world, expelled from the second – the return of this feeling put a spring in her step.

She was a new creature on the bare cement ground. Aliyah looked about her; people were still asleep and there was not a sound to be heard but the howl of dogs – the only sensation that still made her feel connected to the world around her.

For Hanan, the girl's animality was a source of attraction. She would savour the touch of her fingers as they played on her back drawing pictures, and feel a strange sensation at the sight of the servant's dark skin against her own soft white flesh. Meanwhile, Aliyah would feel happiness flow through her as she noticed the mistress's contentment, and she would continue to create new shades. She would be captivated by the colours and the contrast between the differing shades of their skin, as she drew clouds, a donkey, and sometimes roses on her mistress's back. She would build white mountains of foam, which collapsed almost instantly. She laughed, then brought a hand to her mouth, her laughter ceasing. With soapy foam spread over her lips, she turned to her reflection in the mirror, pretending to be an old man. Aliyah laughed raspily, as she drew a great big tree, saying to herself:

'I'm… I'm… Father Christmas.'

It was Mistress Hanan who had introduced her to Father Christmas. Aliyah had seen him on television as she lay by her mistress's side. She had dreamt of him ever since, day and night. Sometimes, when she felt especially happy, she would gather a mound of foam on her chest and turn towards her mistress who, in a state of delirium, grabbed tightly onto the girl's fingers, laughing hysterically. Aliyah would get out of the bath, damp with steam and soapy white foam which hung from her body like marshmallow. Then, she would go to her room to retrieve blank paper and a collection of pens with which she would draw for Hanan the pictures she had sketched on her back. As she drew, Aliyah recalled the soft touch of her mistress's skin and the invigorating scents of the oils and felt as though she were living in a paradise. Her sketches would start at her mistress's neck and end at the base of her back.

Aliyah's senses were reawakened in that colourful, clean place. When she looked out into the distance, her view was no longer obstructed by the walls of the little room as it was back in the alleyway. She would close her eyes and try to believe she really was in a place shaded by trees, where the soft curtains played over the windows and, more importantly, where her father's beatings could not reach. At night, there, she was no longer haunted by her sister's wide-eyed ghost, and the smell of the skips had vanished.

When she was still eleven years old, Aliyah would tremble a little when Hanan al-Hashimi would place her in her lap and make her rub her body with strange oils, her fingers squeezing her quivering skin.

Pliant like dough, Aliyah would give in to the mistress, letting her do as she pleased. In the beginning she had feared her gentle caresses – the source of nightmares that stole her sleep – but day by day, as she grew older in the villa, the mistress's touch became the subject of daydreams; she began to wait for it in anticipation. Aliyah knew now of the precious treasure concealed within her own body, which she could grant her mistress when she felt like it and withhold from her when she was in a bad mood. Yet this was only at night. In the daytime, Aliyah avoided the mistress, keeping a distance as though the woman were poisonous.

Night and day were two quite separate worlds.

Aliyah's fingers froze around the handle of her bag. Sharp twinges ran through them as she struggled to hold her grip on the bag and keep her balance as she walked. As her fingers entwined over the leather skin she teetered on the point of falling. Then, her hand let go and the bag fell. Aliyah felt a chill run through her warm fingers, whose games had made her the queen of a magic realm. She watched the digits tremble, concealing them close to her belly as she wondered to herself what was causing them to shiver like that in summer. Perhaps it was the dawn chill, which arose there as in all desert-like places.

But the cold wasn't so intense as to make her fingers freeze like that; it was fear, she realised. Fear alone had turned her to a lump of ice. Aliyah remembered how her fingers would become completely rigid, refusing to bend or dance as sharp twinges of pain shot through them. It was happening again right then, as she tried to put her hands in her pockets to protect them from the biting chill of the morning. Aliyah studied her fingers. They seemed unfamiliar to her now. Those fingers that had once transformed Hanan al-Hashimi's nights into eternal pleasure, before she had turned her out into this new unknown.

That moment was etched upon her mind: the mistress charging at her like a woman possessed and throwing her out. Every time the memory arose, she shivered and began to falter, like a tattered yellow leaf on a wizened tree branch. Aliyah searched for a single convincing reason to explain why that woman – who was clearly deranged – wore so many different faces, some so frightening that she trembled when Hanan appeared in her dreams and turned into a savage. In bed, Hanan's features were quite different, as if the djinn had taken possession of her. She became like an infant, her eyes shimmering as her body began to relax. In Aliyah's embrace, Hanan was an obedient child. On other occasions, when she had guests, Hanan displayed a third face: her features would drain of colour and their contours turn to broken lines over a face devoid of laughter.

The prickling sensations intensified. Aliyah brought her palms close to her mouth and breathed some warmth into them. Looking behind her once more, she saw nothing of her own world – that world which, until so recently, had been everything she owned. Once more, she picked up her bag and started to run, stumbling in her high-heel shoes. Why she had been so insistent on that particular pair, she did not know. From the clothes she was wearing, Aliyah momentarily imagined she looked like Hanan al-Hashimi, dressed up for one of her soirées from which she wouldn't return until dawn.

She took off the shoes and carried them, running and crying at the top of her voice, just like when she was a little girl. Aliyah dried her tears as she ran. Stumbling, she came to a halt, then charged on once more, without a thought for where she was going. Why was she so terrified? What was she afraid of? She didn't know; she was afraid and that was that. Days which she thought were gone for good came back to her: memories of the times when she would carry a knife close to her thigh, of how her heart would pound as she kept watch over the doorway to the family's little room, where her sister lay.

The sound of tears filled the wide open space as she crossed the terrain on a narrow track, with nothing for company but her fingers, her bag and her fear. And with fear came the memories of al-Raml.

Aliyah jumped at the sound of a car. She was all alone on an empty road, the morning sun having not yet risen. She stopped, looked down and pulled out a sharp knife from her little bag. She held the knife tightly, ready to brandish it in the face of any being, whether they came out of the ground or swooped down from above. But the car didn't stop, or even slow down and she carried recklessly on her way, her heart pounding as the car shot past. In the next moment, silence had returned and the dust settled.

Aliyah sighed. Returning the knife to her bag, she looked back towards the villa. In a daze, she stared out at the expanse before her. She had crossed the terrain so quickly that Hanan's villa seemed like a mirage now. For a brief moment, Aliyah imagined she had never lived there, attempting to gather courage again. Over the years, she had trained herself to be brave, but now she felt shaken. Every part of her body bubbled and fizzed; her chest rose and fell heavily; her stare was as sharp as her knife, which had not left her side since the day her mother had hidden it in her school dress. It was her mother who had taught her how to use the blade to ward off the boys, or the men, who harassed her from time to time in the alley-ways of the red-light district.

Aliyah was not the only girl to be taught how to wield a knife; there were many but unlike the others, she had once brandished hers openly and seen the enchanting way it glistened in the sunlight. Yet her actions that day were not random, nor were they out of bravado.

It had happened on one of the days when the door was left ajar and her siblings had gone out. Aliyah Senior had been left alone in the house to watch the sunlight stream through the gap in the door, to listen to the passing footsteps, the wailing children and their screeching mothers. She didn't notice the shadow suddenly cast over the doorway; it had appeared in the blink of an eye. There was little time to ask the neighbour's son what he was up to, for he shut the door and immediately descended upon the girl. Aliyah felt as though her bones would be crushed under his weight as he gagged her mouth. She flapped beneath him like a fish out of water, but he didn't seem to care. Her face suddenly creased, her hair became tangled about her neck and her limbs began to shake. Aliyah was no longer the beautiful young girl she had once been. Ever since the room had swallowed her up, the neighbour's son had been watching it day and night, waiting for his chance. He had easy access to her now. He lifted her robe up to her navel. What happened after that, the boy wasn't quite sure. Before entering her, he began to shake so violently that everything around him shook too. Aliyah Senior was almost unconscious. She struggled to breathe with his hand covering both her nose and mouth. Had he not started to shake and then fled, without looking into her blue face, she would have suffocated under his weight. On subsequent occasions, the boy would again wait for the family to leave their room. Now he would come with a sharp knife in one hand and gag Aliyah's mouth with the other. He would remove her pants violently and then mount her. The boy had been back dozens of times before Little Aliyah caught him. She had opened the rusty iron door to hear her sister sobbing quietly. She noticed a pair of black buttocks accelerating steadily above where her sister lay and the knife glimmering between Aboud's teeth. Little Aliyah threw down her books and took out her own blade, which was held by a leather belt at the side of her pants. She screamed wildly, as if not knowing how to speak. Then, tearing her school dress, she jumped onto half-naked Aboud, gashing his buttocks until the blood poured and he leapt about the room like an ape. Aliyah clung to Aboud like a small wild animal, lunging with her knife at every part of his body within reach. The boy staggered a little as he attempted to put on his trousers and Aliyah jumped on his back, bit him and brought him to the ground. Had some of the neighbourhood men not managed eventually to extract her, Aliyah would have killed him; her teeth had sunk into his shoulder, staining her little mouth with blood. For a moment, Aliyah's body fused with the boy's. She had reduced him to such shreds that the men imagined they were seeing a wild beast before them.

People in the neighbourhood made fun of Aboud for a long time after. They remembered Little Aliyah too – how she had clung to the boy, whose body dripped with blood where the sharp blade had struck, how she had screamed and swore, then stood with her legs apart, like the neighbourhood bullies, challenging any one of those sons of bitches to even attempt to come close to her crippled sister.

That evening, Aliyah Senior killed herself. She passed away the very same night that everyone discovered what Aboud had been doing to her in her paralysed state. Little Aliyah never went back to her school books, unable to forget what had happened that day. Aliyah couldn't understand why the men didn't pray for her sister as they usually did when burying their dead. Nor did she know why the women shed so many tears as they described the girl's beauty. Her sister's eyes held her captive, open as wide as they would go. She told no one about the yellow container she had given her sister – the one her mother used to spray the floor and the corners of the room, to keep away the rats. Why there was foam pouring from her sister's mouth, she didn't understand. She didn't know where her sister's voice had vanished to either. How would her sister survive underground with the Devil? She wondered for a moment. He had started to come to her in her dreams, sometimes as Aboud, sometimes as her father, occasionally in some other form.

When she woke up from her nightmares, she would pick up her knife and go searching in the dark, grimy alleyways for Aboud, who had disappeared shortly after the incident, not daring to return until Little Aliyah had vanished. He heard the neighbours say that her father had left her to an aristocratic Damascene family and taken her wages for the years ahead.

Aliyah was ten years old at the time. She had left school and joined the group of children who hung around the rubbish skips in certain parts of Damascus. It made no difference to them whether the neighbourhood was rich or poor; their only concern was to collect the empty glass containers, clean them and gather them in plastic bags. Aliyah preferred her new job to staying at home, or having to get up early and walk for miles along the muddy tracks to school.

Hanan al-Hashimi had turned Aliyah's life on its head. She had cleansed her of her old self and purged her fears; she had removed every layer of anger and rubbed away the images of al-Raml with her fingers. But now they returned in full, not a single detail missing. All at once, the images settled in her mind, urging her at one moment to flee, but more often to halt.

With small, pained footsteps, Hanan staggered between the window and the corners of the room. She worried about her maid, who would surely be in danger if she went beyond the zone of the villas.

'If only she'd just come back!' Hanan took a deep breath as she tried to think of a way to make Aliyah return without sacrificing her own pride… She would make the gardener go out to look for her. Then she remembered Anwar, whom she had left to bathe in indifference. Hanan laughed snidely. That old crocodile wouldn't be able to help her; he was still lying stiff on his mattress and hadn't made the slightest sound.

She so wanted him to die! That parasite. He'd been sucking away at her life all that time, since their very first night together. She had never loved him. That man who had once been a brother to her, then a cousin, then husband. Now, in this final form of his, he was her old crocodile.

The crocodile would put his hand over her mouth, telling her to be quiet as he mounted her. He would stay there in silence a few minutes then get up, wash and curl back into his shell. Hanan was growing up, reaching the prime of her youth, whilst Anwar was becoming an old man. He would spend hours settling his peculiar business deals – drinking vodka and fiddling with his gilt prayer beads. Hanan quickly became attuned to his social circles and accompanied him when he was invited to parties or for dinner at other business-men's houses. There, the men would always sit in a separate room to the women. Sometimes Hanan spent her mornings with the wives of Anwar's colleagues and acquaintances. She never thought about whether she was happy or not. The way the wives behaved often irritated her, but she was obliged by her husband to flatter them and invite them over for dinner. Anwar's friends were all share-holders in a number of compa-nies based in Syria, Lebanon or Jordan and most were govern-ment ministers or prominent businessmen.

Hanan started taking part in charity benefits and attending gatherings with the other upper-class women, mostly at the house of Amina, an older lady who lived in al-Malki. The rest of the time she spent visiting her friends in their homes and hosting members of the family on their short visits back to the homeland. All the while, Hanan observed her husband's growing prosperity. At times, she felt a little intimidated by his acquaintances; they were the people you only ever saw on television, or perhaps only their name was familiar. She was bored. Bored of them and bored by her whole existence, but it was no longer within her power to sacrifice everything she'd gained: the stability, the high society gatherings where she roamed like a spoilt princess, her manic impulses to shop. She could have anything she wanted. Anything that was, except for a child. Hanan had travelled to the four corners of the earth in search of an embryo to nurture in her womb, but always returned disappointed. Yet when she got to know Nazek at those dinner parties, her life was turned on its head. She began to understand what it was to wait for dawn, to jump out of bed with the pleasurable prospect of leaving the confines of her house. Her husband had told her repeatedly to please Nazek and to get to know her well. It wasn't long before the lady in question approached Hanan, taking a clear interest in her and inviting her over for a visit.

That first evening at Nazek's took place before Hanan had discovered her little treasure, exposed by Aliyah's fingers. That evening, Nazek made each of her guests their own drink. When asked for her drink of choice, Hanan al-Hashimi stuttered; she had never tasted alcohol before. 'Vodka and lemon,' she said, feeling a little dazed as she spoke, hearing the sound of her own voice resonate in the air. 'Vodka and lemon.' Why didn't she tell Nazek that she didn't drink? Hanan took the glass. It would be her little secret, she decided. No need for Anwar to know.

Nazek had a rasping voice and wore a thin, white cotton jacket and a pair of dark jeans. On her feet were a pair of elegant slippers, yet her body was bare of any jewellery. Nazek seemed younger than her age as she wandered the room, hopping about like a hungry rabbit and showering Hanan with attention. Every now and then, she would leave Hanan's side and return with strange yet delicious samples of food, holding out one tray as she waited for Hanan to taste, then inclining a little before Hanan as she presented her with another. Hanan was embarrassed by the hostess's overwhelming attentiveness. The other women too showered her with praise, complimenting her beauty and the style of her hair, which was cut short. Hanan didn't feel irritated as she usually did at the gatherings she attended under duress from her husband. Normally, she would be obliged to lower her voice while the men stared at her hungrily and made her feel uncomfortable. Without knowing why, she always felt as if she were suffocating. Sweet shudders took over her body whenever she met a man's eye. Engrossed in his gaze, she would feel the piercing shine slice her heart in two and send a tremor through every limb of her body. She would be dying to run away, to escape her shameful shivers.

In female company, Hanan was more at ease. Men had a tendency to shake her feminine sensibilities, but there, amongst women, it was like walking in a soft, silken dream. Hanan showered her host with compliments, feeling that she could trust her, that Nazek could read her broken heart.

The other women left Nazek to be with her guest undisturbed, colluding with her perhaps, as their glimmering eyes watched from a distance. The four women were all between the ages of forty and fifty, although they seemed younger. Hanan was taken aback by the way they drank, gulping down liquor as if it were water. She found it difficult to believe these were the same women who attended engagements with their husbands; they seemed completely different.

The wild glimmer in the women's eyes exaggerated their beauty. Later, Hanan would come to understand from the lessons Nazek gave as she lay in her arms.

'There's something more beautiful, more sensitive about women, something that makes you shine. It's different with men – you get all sorts. Some you want to shut in your room for days and screw to exhaustion, but then outside the bedroom they don't mean a thing to you. Then there are the ones you dream about spending your whole life just talking and flirting with; here the pleasure is in staying just within the limits. There are the men who make you want to cry in their arms, and others you sit with and discuss the ways of the world, inside-out. But with women, love is different. When passion takes hold of you and you're completely absorbed in your lover's kiss, she is all of those men in one: a lover, a friend and an everlasting object of desire. Women are more sensitive to everything, believe me. Men are boorish, even if they appear otherwise. In your arms, a woman is like silk; she gives away her heart before giving her body. A man would never do that.'

Hanan had started to throw the past behind her, she realised. There was no hope of turning back now, no hope of going back to the start. The women turned into butterflies before her eyes: where did that joy in their movements come from? Light radiated around each of them like a halo as they gravitated towards each other, laughing sweetly, floating in a weightless space.

One of the women, Leena, was the wife of a military officer. Leena was strikingly beautiful, her complexion not white exactly, but more the fair, rosy tone characteristic of most women from the Syrian coast. Thanks to her rural origins, Leena was the least malicious of the women and took delight in teasing the Damascenes, that they were bastards. The Damascene women found little objection to her use of the word, as Leena told them the story of Tamerlane's sacking of Damascus

– how he had taken the women as prisoners and left them to his soldiers, who had raped them for days, spawning generations of illegitimate offspring. From that time onwards the children of Damascus became known as bastards. The women laughed at Leena's anecdote, one retorting that the servant girls of each of their grandmothers had been simpletons from the coast with lice-infested hair, who spread their legs at night for their masters. Leena laughed in return, not in the least offended.

The second woman of the group was the wife of a factory owner whose company produced cleaning products. She wore an elegant headscarf in a fashionable style, but her dress sense was quite peculiar, the vibrant colours of her clothes giving her the look of a moving garden.

Maha, the third woman, was thin and silent and moved anxiously, preoccupied in smoking her cigarettes. Maha spoke with a strange accent, the result of having grown up in Aleppo and marrying in Damascus. At her soirées in Aleppo, where the other women in their intimate circle came together, her attentiveness matched Nazek's. In time, Hanan got to know those women too, at the evenings she was invited to by Nazek. Most of the girls had married young and each one of them had a female lover. Very few people knew exactly what was going on, since their gatherings were monopolised by women, and the men felt quite secure when their wives were in female company, even if there was something unsettling about their friendship. So long as the relationship remained a secret, there was no problem, but as soon as rumours started, the husband would sever the relationship between his wife and her companion.

Many of the women at these ladies' gatherings were of the rich Aleppan elite. Nazek went to great lengths to ensure that

Hanan would not become overly acquainted with any of them, afraid that with their skills of seduction one might snatch Hanan to be her lover.

The fourth woman at the gathering was a mysterious figure, wearing only a svelte dress which began at the top of her bust and ended just above her knee. Nazek said little about the woman to Hanan, although she showed her great affection, calling her not by her own name but by an honorific moniker: Umm al-Nour, Mother of Light.

Hanan was afraid. As she sipped the vodka her insides burned from her throat right down to the tips of her toes. A few sips were enough for her to feel a fire inside. She was dazed and happy; for the first time she had discovered what joy felt like, listening to the women's obscene jokes.

'They're happy,' she said to Nazek, sipping her vodka.

'More than happy,' Nazek replied, attempting to read Hanan.

'I'm jealous.' Hanan put down her glass and lowered her head in defeat.

'You're not happy yourself? I can't imagine a single woman who deserves happiness more than you do.'

'I don't know,' Hanan responded, wanting some time to consider Nazek's words. 'What is happiness?' she went on. 'Contentment? Satisfaction?'

'In simple terms, happiness is doing what we want to do. But actually it's a lot more complicated than that; you know yourself that nobody gets the happiness they wish for.'

'The happiness that *who* wishes for? Me? You? Them?' Hanan asked, as Nazek enveloped her in her gaze. She examined every detail of Hanan, like a bird of prey about to swoop in for the kill. Yet as Nazek's eyes devoured her, Hanan remained perfectly at ease, unfazed.

'Do you trust that this is your happiness? It might only be temporary, but it's still happiness... laughing and joking and making our loved ones happy.' Nazek moved closer and trailed her warm fingers across Hanan's forehead. As Hanan pulled away, Nazek withdrew her fingers and carried on talking, leaning into Hanan's face.

'Hanan my dove. As delicate as can be.'

Hanan was bringing back to mind those moments of her surrender to Nazek, happy at having found something to occupy her thoughts other than the maid she had sent away. Yet this contentment barely lasted a second moment before turning to deep sorrow. Hanan had remembered how little she had meant to Nazek. Of course, she wasn't as insignificant as a servant, but at best Nazek had strung her along. It was Nazek who had preyed on her, Nazek who had acquainted her with her hesitancy, and later her delight; with Aliyah, however, she was the mistress morning, noon and night. Wasn't it she, Hanan, who directed the girl's fingers to the zones of pleasure? She'd been the one to give the first orders, hadn't she? Even if Aliyah had started to act the mistress later on, she only did so because she knew what her mistress wanted.

Hanan recollected just how fragile she had felt, lost amongst those women, her look of confusion the same as the look she found later in Aliyah's eyes as she undressed before the girl. From within her ribs, despair erupted like hot steam from a fountain.

Hanan could picture the outfit she had worn that evening with complete clarity: an elegant Chanel dress concealed beneath her brown *jilbab* and matched with a pair of heels. She had sat alone on a sofa set apart from the others, her right leg crossed over the left. Shaking away her lethargy, she got up and started to cross the room, moving coyly to the sound of the music. Hanan had caught the women's attention – so perfect in her coffee-coloured shoes and dress, which matched the colour of her hijab and *jilbab*, bracelets, necklace, earrings and her handbag. The contrast of her milky-white skin against the earthen brown tone gave her the look of a miniature porcelain doll or the perfect children pictured in fashion magazines. Hanan laughed aloud and swallowed the last sip of her drink as Nazek approached, waving her glass.

'Whiskey tastes much nicer.'

Hanan meandered seductively, trembling as the lady kissed her forehead. She laughed. 'I prefer vodka.'

The lady laughed too and put her arms around Hanan. For a few moments, Hanan was paralysed. Then to her own surprise and that of her hostess alike, she drew her face close and whispered in her ear, 'I want another glass.'

Nazek took hold of Hanan's glass and squeezed her hand, sending a shiver running through Hanan's body from the centre of her head down to the base of her spine. Hanan closed her eyes and when she opened them again, the lady was staggering happily towards her. She sat down beside Hanan on the edge of the sofa. There was a levity in the way the women's shadows moved, and the way their arms curved and bent towards one another, which hadn't been so apparent before. Hanan could make out from the movements each body's longing to roll into a ball and scarper, to avoid collision. The bodies drew close, then moved apart, wanting to touch and be touched. They backed away, they played little tricks; each woman wanted to make her own torso the centre of movement, twisting and turning, bending parallel to the floor where their feet stamped.

Hanan was captivated by the way the women moved; with their eyes closed they were gone from the world, yet every limb of their bodies danced in perfect harmony. She wondered if her body would obey her if she danced, but didn't dare to try. The women's animation sent the blood dancing through her veins. She tried copying them, raising her arm until it fell and she was convinced that, were she to stop in response to the blood careering beneath her skin, she would certainly lose her balance. From the corner opposite to where she was sitting Nazek beckoned. Hanan struggled to stand up, as though something heavy were pinning her down. She saw nothing but the woman's piercing eyes; everything else was a blur. Slowly pacing across the room, she forgot about the other women. Hanan's coyness had driven the hostess wild. Coming close to Hanan, she grabbed her hand by the tips of her fingers and led her towards the bedroom.

The room had three sides, like a triangular hollow, and a generous free-standing mattress occupied the space. The bed was deep red in colour and scattered with miniature cushions, which spilled over onto the floor. Music floated down from the ceiling into the warm air. On a glass bedside table in the shape of a heart were several glasses and two gold-rimmed cups; one had a long neck, the other one shorter. To the side of the glasses was an assortment of women's menthol cigarettes.

Nazek shut the door. Hanan's heart was pounding so hard that she felt her body were about to explode. There was that scent again; it filled the air as Nazek approached. She stood silently as Nazek removed her dress. Mistress Nazek then stripped herself and the two women stood face-to-face.

Hanan looked out from the gap in the curtains once more, expecting to see Aliyah making her way back. She watched like a hunter awaiting his hawk's return and tried not to think of the night she had become Nazek's prey. But the powerful scent wafting in the air had brought with it the memory of Nazek's touch as she had undressed her.

Hanan pictured Aliyah naked. The girl was gone. She could no longer smell her scent in the air. The realisation made her panic. If only she'd been a little less harsh. She could have dragged her to her room, locked the door and given her a beating. She could have cried and pleaded with her to explain her betrayal. Or perhaps she should have hit Anwar instead, for meddling with her little girl?

She could see Nazek's expression as it had been in those moments when the lady undressed her, turning her into another woman. The face appeared in confrontation with Aliyah's, attacking and chastising it until Hanan gave a loud snort and batted her arms in the air to make the vision disappear.

'What have I done wrong?' she croaked softly. Hanan slapped her face with both hands. She stood with her body frozen perfectly still, whilst in her mind she returned to that night at Nazek's.

What had happened for the scent to torture her like that? That scent of Nazek's menthol cigarettes from all those years ago – the mint fragrance which had transformed into cinnamon. Back then, Hanan would escape with her little housesparrow. She soaked up the fragrance as Nazek played with her body, covering her in kisses. The moment the lady's fingers slipped between her thighs, a shudder ran through Hanan's body. Her nostrils flared and she closed her eyes, her head resting in Nazek's hands. Nazek was startled as she watched Hanan's face crease in pain. How could a woman's orgasm be so agonising? she wondered. And how could Hanan reach climax from her kisses and caresses alone?

The scent of cinnamon took Hanan back to her maid's slender body. Hanan – in her prime – was the ship's captain, leading Aliyah's fingers wherever she pleased, before she vanished under a drape of hot, foamy water.

∾

The streak of light faded into nothingness.

The light which had led Hanan to discover that the girl had slipped into Anwar's room, the light which had sent Aliyah scurrying like a lizard under her feet – that same light waned until it had vanished completely beneath the blinding rays of the rising sun.

∾

Aliyah put her bag down on the side of the road. She sat down on top of it, resting as she waited for the rubbish truck which always came at that time of morning and would take her into the city. She took off the gold chain from around her neck and slipped it into her pocket; it would be down to her to protect it from greedy hands. Aliyah took a deep breath in preparation for the stench of the rubbish. The scent of the mansion houses was different to the rotten odour that she had lived with for so many months, that had lingered in her nostrils until Hanan's fingers and the scent of cinnamon tea had washed away all the scents that came before.

The putrid odour of rubbish returned. Aliyah smiled sorrowfully as she recollected her first day of work in the skips. She had worn her best clothes: a pair of blue jeans and a pink shirt.

She had combed her hair and pulled it tightly into a short plait, before setting off to her friends' house, where a group of children was waiting to set out on the daily rounds.

The boy in charge was waiting for them in a large warehouse, a building of endless depth which carried on up to where the tin shacks began. Although it was only a store for rubbish and glass, nevertheless, it was the best-constructed building in the neighbourhood. There were others like it; the factory owners had taken to setting up their storage spaces there, where they charged the local children with the task of running them.

Before the groups set out to different parts of the city, they gathered around the warehouse supervisor, a boy of about fifteen nicknamed Suzuki by his friends; a name taken from a cartoon ninja hero. Suzuki's hair was shaved into a strip along the centre of his head, in the European style, or so he liked to boast. Carrying pen and paper, he wrote down the names of the children to be split into groups and scattered across different areas of the city. When Aliyah arrived with her two constant companions the boy's eyes shone. Three genies. There were happy days ahead, he thought, as he watched the girls hopping about like bunnies.

The five girls and ten boys would be split into groups of three by Suzuki. The children were to meet at half past twelve in front of the large warehouse on the south side of the quarter. The warehouse was close to Aliyah's school, which made her feel a little uneasy since she would always spot some of her friends. Aliyah was silent as she listened to the instructions. When one of the boys grabbed her by the arm the little remaining joy she felt seemed to disappear.

'I'm group captain!' the boy shouted.

He blew his nose, shivering from the cold. Aliyah stared at

the boy's chapped face, trying to work out who he was. Her friend – the stout girl bodyguard – informed her that the boy was one of those she had bitten the day of the chocolate fiasco. Aliyah felt wary when she realised who he was and made a firm resolution not to get into any fights.

Every day, Suzuki accompanied a different group. They would usually find him waiting for them in front of the workshop, smoking his *narghile* pipe. Aliyah would arrive with her stout little friend and another boy two or three years older than herself who would lead them through the neighbourhoods to the skips. Parading in front of the two girls like a cockerel, he would jubilantly issue orders to them to enter one area or another, to turn left or right. The money that the boy earnt, and the terrible smells – which never left him, even in his sleep – were of little significance in comparison to the joy he felt in the girls' company. The boy was a friend to Aliyah and her companion and she would have liked them to stay together, if only Suzuki would refrain from reorganising the groups.

On her first day with the cockerel boy, Aliyah rummaged through the black sacks of rubbish, scattering them across the pavement. She couldn't find a single container, neither plastic nor glass. She rummaged through the debris, coughing and snorting until the boy came to show her how to sort the glass containers and how to extract useful items from amongst the rubbish – old shoes, hair brushes, dishes and spoons, clothes still good enough to wear. They boy jumped up into the rubbish skip and told the girls to follow. When Aliyah refused he grabbed her hand.

'You've got to learn the art of rummaging; it'll be your lifeline,' he said. After jumping into the green skip, Aliyah felt as if she were in a grave. She struggled to breathe as she watched the boy's black hands delve into the filth.

Aliyah felt her stomach heave, remembering how she had vomited in the skip. She tried to throw up now, standing away from her bag; the taste of acid rose from her stomach into her throat, before sinking back down again. She was shivering, even though the rising sun had started to give out its warmth.

She returned to sit on the bag. Every now and then a dust storm arose, churned up by a passing car. Each time, she jumped but the cars passed by without paying her the slightest attention. The stench of rubbish returned to her mind without the truck ever arriving. Aliyah recollected how the boy had jumped in alarm, swearing at her. He stood on the pavement listening to her coughing violently, hearing her vomit. Seeing what was happening, the other girl reached out a hand to Aliyah and attempted to pull her from the skip. It was hopeless. With her eyes bulging from their sockets, Aliyah was stuck where she was.

Despite everything that had happened, Aliyah remembered the contentment she had known in those days. The burden of school had been lifted from her shoulders and she no longer had to deal with the children calling her the cleaner's daughter. She recalled her mother's faint smile at finally having somebody to help her. Aliyah loved to see her mother laugh; she was so much more beautiful, so much more youthful when she laughed. Yet things were far from perfect. On more than one occasion, Aliyah returned from work crying, with her clothes in tatters as she wiped away the tears and the dirty streaks her fingers had drawn on her face. She never dared to tell her mother what had happened, but her mother understood without need for explanation once she caught sight of the blade in her daughter's hand. Aliyah would remain stationed for hours in front of the door to the family's room, her hands clasped tightly around the blade. She watched the alleyway, ready to leap up at any moment, to bite or to attack in whatever way her anger dictated. She was wary of going out with boys who were bigger than her, knowing what they liked to do to little girls.

Suzuki was tall and dark as pitch, with a pug nose and hair that curled into tight rings. There was something unattractive about the boy picking his nose and leaping about pretending to be a cartoon hero. Suzuki behaved as if he were king and could do as he pleased with the girls, terrorising them with the knife he kept in the waistband of his trousers. He heard about Aliyah's fights with the boys, who told him firmly that he would run into difficulty if he tried to treat Aliyah as he did the other girls. Suzuki put the idea to the back of his mind and the first time he accompanied her, he simply played his role as captain and ignored her completely. Aliyah was wary of Suzuki; she had noticed his piercing glances when the group lined up for him to count the containers they had each collected and receive their share of the money.

When her turn came Aliyah opened her bag, ignoring Suzuki's intentional stroke of the hand as he counted the containers. One time he drew close to her, pressing himself against her back as he pretended to help her lift down the rubbish sack, but Aliyah had jolted away and thrown the bag to the ground. Suzuki pretended not to notice what had happened as the other children sniggered. He waited a while after that before going out with Aliyah's group a second time. He had decided he would break her, or so he told his friends.

The boy in their group that day was skinny and red-faced, his hair was thinning in the middle and singed at the ends from evenings spent in the graveyard smoking with the other local boys. This was Suzuki's right-hand man, his collaborator in touring about the city skips. The moment Suzuki chose him to accompany Aliyah and the other girl, the boys knew what was to happen.

Once the group had moved far out of al-Raml, Suzuki signalled with a wink to his companion, who turned down an alleyway after the other girl, while he continued straight on, puffing out his chest as he moved towards a narrow corner between the wall and the skip. Terrified, Aliyah walked behind the boy, grasping at her knife. She hoped Suzuki could not sense her fear as she heard the screech of her own grinding teeth. Aliyah trembled. For a second, as Suzuki asked her to open the bags thrown behind the skip, she thought perhaps she had made a mistake. Relaxing, she bent down to open the bags and in that very moment, Suzuki accosted her from behind, gagging her.

Suzuki threw her to the ground and tied her arms behind her back like a rope. Even though Aliyah felt as though her bones were about to break, she couldn't scream. The boy yanked down her pants and threw his whole weight onto her. She felt as though she were being crushed beneath him. Aliyah almost choked as she felt his hot, hard member rubbing against her. Had he carried on another minute, she would have died by his hands just like her sister before her, but not a whole moment had passed before she felt the liquid trickling down her inner thigh. Suzuki stopped and pulled up his trousers, holding his knife between his teeth as he drew close to her.

'One word and I'll break you in two!' he threatened before spitting on her. For a few moments Aliyah died. When she closed her eyes the sound of her pounding heart had disappeared. She had seized up. Her bottom half was cold and the smell of the rubbish bags on which she was lying had found its way to her nose.

That day, Aliyah returned home and washed without letting the knife out of her hand. When her mother asked what had happened she said she'd fallen into a pile of rubbish. The following morning, Aliyah went back to work as normal and waited for the right moment. When it came, she assailed Suzuki from behind with the knife, carving deep gashes into his face which left scars that time would never erase. That day she fled the warehouse and never returned to work in the rubbish skips. She stayed at home after that, not taking a step outside again until the day her father took her to Mistress Hanan's house in Muhajireen.

This had all happened when she was still only ten years old.

Aliyah recalled the old scratches on her face from Suzuki's fingernails. When she touched where they had been, the marks had vanished, but there was no need for her to see them to remember. Aliyah felt as though she were back in the alleyways, and for a moment she forgot everything that had happened that night. She could hear Aboud screaming out to the neighbours and, in some deep, secret part of her memory, she fought to tear his image to pieces. A stifled sob blocked her throat. The blood was careering around her body and her fingers trembled as she peered behind her. She knew exactly where the sound was coming from. It was the moan of her beautiful sister, who was alive within her, who had taken possession of her body and soul.

Aliyah stopped and looked out towards the horizon. From somewhere above, she heard the sound of a car. The silence was oppressive. She picked up her bag once more and tottered onwards on her high heels.

∼

Hanan thought about waking Anwar up to go looking for Aliyah.

Daylight streamed in from behind the curtains. Picking herself up off the bathroom floor, she immediately wanted to sit back down again. After hesitating she made her way back to bed, biting her nails and muttering to herself. She might kill him, she mumbled, rather than send him looking for Aliyah.

Hanan's hatred for her husband gradually faded. From beneath her ribs her mother crawled out and took her position in the mirror. Multiple faces peered out at her, each carrying the same expression of anger.

Hanan hid under the sheets. At once the memory came back to her of the first shiver she had felt take hold of her body. She was at the bathhouse. It was the first time she had tasted cinnamon tea, the first time she ever inhaled its scent.

On that early morning, Hanan had held her mother's hand as they walked slowly along a street paved with gleaming black stone. The road ran alongside the Old City wall and Hanan could hear the roar of the water running through the ducts nearby. Little alleys branched off into narrower quarters. There were arches of all sizes, stone walls and decaying *moucharaby* windows. Once they had skirted the length of the stone wall, the wide square appeared before them, filled with orange trees, rose bushes and jasmine, the scents transforming the city evenings into a perfumed dream which cloaked the ugliness. As her nose recollected the fragrance, Hanan's memory of her first visit to the women's bathhouse came back to her. It was the wedding day of the neighbour's daughter.

The bride was of medium build and full-bodied. Eight years older than Hanan, she visited their house frequently with her mother, Hajja Husniya al-Miwalidi, and always wearing a black *aba*. Yet that morning, the bride was sitting beside the large stone basin while two of the female attendants rubbed her back and her mother roamed the room with a censer. The incense fused with the scents of the women's bodies, the bay soap and olive hair treatment, as the figures moved like ghosts through the thick steam. Naked, the women were like divine creations, their hair flowing down as they called out to each other coquettishly with little screams and shouts, taking furtive glances at the bride's body to quench their curiosity. Their observations would be the basis of much discussion on future Damascus mornings: how round were her buttocks? Were her hips wide enough to bear healthy infants? Were her breasts full or flaccid? What about the feel of her skin, was it soft? Were her thighs strong and in proportion? Did she smell sweet?

Each body has its own odour, and it was down to the groom's mother to take the bride in her arms and capture her scent time and again. The fact that most women with Damascene origins had similar looks – pale skin and curvaceous figures – meant nothing to the family members of a prospective bride, who would bring their sixteen-year-old daughter to the bathhouse, her soft white body not yet fully developed. There the girl would provide a spectacle for the onlookers and the women would pinch every part of her body, winking at her and paying compliments. Eyes would follow the girl as she moved about slowly and seductively, while the women would imagine what she would be like in the groom's bed. That day, Hanan was amongst the girls whose role it was to accompany the bride as she bathed for the last time before her wedding night, the night of consummation.

At the bathhouse, Hanan was alarmed by her own nakedness. She tried to copy her mother, who was busy smoking *narghile* with some of the other women in the busy inner courtyard. In that moment, Hanan too became captivated by the bride, following her every move as she considered the meaning of the women's words and the glimmer in their eyes. When she stepped out of the inner chamber, the women teased Hanan, beckoning her to sit next to the bride. Anxious, Hanan looked over from the edge of the room towards her mother, who motioned to her from afar to return inside, laughing from her spot in the centre of the women, where she sat as if she were their queen. Hanan returned to sit beside the bride, who ordered a cup of cinnamon tea.

She remembered how the women had laughed at the bride's request, and how the bride had blushed with embarrassment, asking the women to back away a little and to pay attention, since their nails had left marks on her body. Later in life, Hanan would learn that sticks of cinnamon, like those which her mother put in the kettle when she made tea for the family, worked magic on a bride, giving her greater strength to bear the man's desires in their marriage bed. At this pre-nuptial bathing ceremony, the bride became aware that her request was a cause for embarrassment, as she recalled the reputation of cinnamon. The fuss was not about to die down peacefully and the bride sought refuge in a corner of the bathhouse, far from the women's stealthy glances. Barely opening her eyes, the bride asked Hanan to stay by her side. She took her by the hand and gently stroked her back, before lifting her onto her lap. The girl laughed, telling Hanan that she was a mischievous little thing. She spoke to her sweetly about the trips their families had taken together to Ghouta and about the devilish tricks of the boys hiding behind the apricot trees. Then she released her, letting her slip into the stone tub, where she began massaging her body with a strange, perfumed mud.

When the cup of tea arrived, the two girls laughed and the scent of cinnamon filled the air. From her spot below, Hanan peered at the large woman who had brought the tea. She couldn't make out her head; all she saw was a great lump of flesh dangling over her. When the woman turned around, her buttocks shook. The little girl stared at her greedily as the bride laughed out loud.

'Mount Qasyoun's moving,' whispered the bride in the little girl's ear. Hanan giggled shyly as the bride pulled her closer, covering her back with mud as she shouted for a second cup of tea.

'Delicious with the steam. Tea is nothing without cinnamon,' she whispered, her eyes fixed on Hanan, who had started to shiver.

The bride sipped her tea slowly, taking in the scent – the cinnamon fragrance blended with the steam and hot water, the laurel oil and the mud covering her body. Hanan wanted to go to sleep; she felt as though everything was calling her to take a little nap amongst the brouhaha. When the bride realised that the neighbour's daughter had started to nod off she slipped down to the side of the stone tub and started to splash the girl's body with the warm water, rubbing her thighs. The glimmer in Hanan's eyes grew stronger and she clung to the bride, wrapping her arms around her, startled by the abrupt awakening.

Hanan began to sense a white shadow creeping into view. The bride pulled Hanan's trembling hand away from her waist and placed it over her right breast. A large pink nipple lay between the little fingers. Hanan's fingers remained frozen in place. She wanted to scream, not understanding anything that was happening. She must be dreaming, she thought, until the bride's moans told her she was awake. The head of the moving flesh mountain was peering down above her. The matron put the warm cup of tea next to the basin and left. The bride picked it up and brought it to Hanan's trembling lips, pulling the girl swiftly towards her. As she did so, Hanan caught a glimpse of the bride's deepest spot – the part that women are supposed to keep hidden, to guard more closely than their own life. As her mother would often say:

'A girl holds her life in one hand, and this in the other...'

Could she recall what her mother used to say about how that triangular space where her legs met her body was both a blessing and a curse? It could be the rope used to hang her or the lasso she used to capture a man. The triangle nestling between the bride's legs seemed perfectly shaped, toy-like. Hanan closed her eyes but the bride pulled her towards her, to sit in her lap. All of a sudden, the bride stopped and scooped Hanan up briskly. Hanan gave a faint yelp, feeling fire burning in her veins and a stinging pain where the bride was pressing. The bride grabbed her by her buttocks, pulling her thighs apart as she moved her about violently. A suppressed moan issued from the bride's lips and in that instant Hanan felt a tremor take over her body. The potent scent rising from the warm cup stole her away from the world and Hanan fell onto the stone floor unconscious.

When she woke up, Hanan was unsure what had happened. The bride was occupied with plucking the remaining fine hairs from her stomach and the women had gone to rub their bodies with strange oils and mud. Everything had returned to how it had been before, except that Hanan was wrapped up in towels, trembling with fear as she lay stretched out on the stone bench beside her mother, who was peering at her worriedly as she continued to exhale smoke. The women spattered Hanan's body with a vile, pungent perfume which made her cough. Hanan searched the air for that newly discovered scent. Later she would come to know it as her first scent and her last.

That evening, Hanan walked beside the bride in an embroidered white skirt. She felt as though what had happened in the bathhouse was pulling her irrationally towards the bride, but Hanan's attempts to attract her attention were futile and her distress brought her to tears.

Hanan tried to recall the morning she had spent with that mysterious creation Aliyah. The scent of bitter orange, of roses and jasmine, which had once cloaked all the ugly things, no longer filled the air but wafted from her memory. Hanan grabbed Aliyah's hand on the way to the women's bathhouse and it was as though time had stood still. Other than the alterations to the shop fronts and the trading stalls dotted along the pavements, the alleyways were just as they had been then, but now the river had run dry and the city wall of Damascus with its seven doors seemed different.

Aliyah walked on without letting go of Hanan's fingers. She unclenched her fist to reveal a pitch-black palm with so many creases it looked like the hand of a fifty-year-old. Hanan took out a handkerchief and placed it in the girl's hand, then carried on walking until she reached the bathhouse – that same place where she had once sat beneath the domed roof. This time, Hanan noticed things that had escaped her attention as a nine-year-old: the walls were decorated with blue drawings, enamel roses and tree branches; in the centre of the room was a small pool, inlayed with marble and coloured mother-of-pearl, with a great water fountain springing up in the middle. On the sides of the pool were rows of potted plants – carnations, gillyflowers and snapdragons. Raised stone benches ran along the sides of the walls, covered with wide cushions and scattered with pillows, like a royal chamber. *Narghile* pipes made of blue Damascene glass were placed along the platforms, surrounded by stones on which the women could sit to smoke after bathing, their torsos wrapped in towels.

The woman who ran the bathhouse sat in the centre of the room behind a wide table, where she monitored what was happening, shouting orders and welcoming her customers as the women led their girls in for the others to examine, hoping to find them a husband once the women started their analysis of the girls during the bathing session.

The girls lined up with their mothers and sisters, choosing a stone basin which they shared between two, each massaging the other and taking turns to cover their partner's body with a soft clay that strengthened the skin. In the corner of the room, the masseuses waited to rub the women's backs with a coarse, black mitt which would remove the dirt and open the pores of their skin.

Everybody was naked. Hanan had discovered that women were all more beautiful without their clothes than they were in their black *jilbabs*. Often, the masseuses would speak foully as they exfoliated the women's bodies. Some of the women enjoyed listening silently to the masseuses' bawdy conversations among the cloud of steam and the clamour of voices. From the warm basin, Hanan observed what was happening around her. It was as if she were dreaming, her hand leading Aliyah's fingers left and right, over her nipples, and down below her stomach.

That scent – the one she had locked away in her heart for decades – had returned with the little servant girl, who had overturned her authority and thrown her into torment.

Hanan observed her own image in the mirror, putting a hand to her mouth just as Aliyah used to do. She ran down to the bedroom on the ground floor and quietly pushed open the door. Her husband was there in his pyjamas, his death-like scent filling the air. Hanan crept towards him on the tips of her toes. As she stared into his face, she felt a fading hatred. Then she left the room, her heart pounding like a drum.

'She betrayed me with a decrepit crocodile.'

Hanan spoke the words clearly, hearing the sound of her own voice as she watched her tears. Now, for the first time in her life, she had discovered the taste of betrayal.

Aliyah's steps grew heavier as she continued along the wide road. Even though the sun had risen, she still hadn't spotted a single person; nobody to make her feel safe. The place was empty but for the barking of dogs from behind the villa walls and the anguished howls of other frightened strays.

Tiredness had worn her down and the bag had started to feel even heavier now. Every few minutes she looked behind her, catching a glimpse of the few remaining shadows; nothing but emptiness. She combatted her fear with the taste of victory, contemplating how bitterness had assailed her mistress like a storm.

Aliyah felt the prick of needles slowly piercing her skin, from her knees to the tips of her fingers. She turned towards the nearest villa, which was surrounded by tall, dark-green cypress trees. Choosing a spot clear of fresh grass, she threw down her bag, collapsed beneath the tree and took off her heels, flinging them away in disgust. She stretched out her legs and leant her head back, hitting it against a tree root. Aliyah winced and closed her eyes. Her body was like a sticky mass suspended in the air, she thought. Her eyes burned and her fingers were fading away. She felt her heart leave her chest and slip from her body through her fingers.

Aliyah still couldn't quite believe that the mistress had sent her away. For a long time, she had been convinced that the mistress's love for her was so strong that she couldn't possibly live without her. She was certain that the tears she had seen in her eyes were genuine, that her mistress was still sensitive to her kisses, to the touch of her fingers as they caressed her or bathed her body, as they washed her hair or lingered between her thighs, massaging her with oil and dousing her with perfume. She would brush her mistress's hair, kissing her eyes as she held her in her arms. The nights when she left her mistress's room limping from the pain in her hips, her face swollen where she'd been bitten, were over. Aliyah found it hard to swallow. She was pleased with what she had done to her mistress; a sense of delight would come over her whenever she sensed her mistress's desire for her. She had imagined the feeling would last forever.

When she first began to work in her mistress's service Aliyah was suspicious of the woman, who would come home late at night and scuttle about at the ends of the house as though she were lost, clattering and clanging until morning came. She would wake up before sunrise and sit sipping her coffee and chattering on the telephone, complaining about her family, cursing her crocodile husband and ruing the day she had first set eyes on him. Yet when she had guests, Hanan was a woman of calm and reserve.

Aliyah would stalk Hanan about the house curiously, snooping on her from behind the curtains or through the keyhole. She would leap like a monkey from one object to another, disappearing behind the furniture whenever Hanan spotted her. She dreaded having to stay with the cook in one place. Instead, Aliyah would take her food, wrap it in a special handkerchief and eat her dinner while sitting on the floor beside the bed. She was too shy to eat in the presence of others.

Day after day, Aliyah waited tirelessly for her father to arrive, or her mother. Head in hands, she sat on the stone steps, her sight fixed on the iron gate. She would stay there as still as a block of dry wood, until Hanan called for her. Aliyah stared at a spot in space, which became a great stage before her eyes. Her mother moved across it like a doll, calling her, chastising her, shouting. Aliyah's face swelled with muted anger. In a distant, shadowy corner, she could make out a small bed. From it there came a sobbing sound and she could just distinguish the shape of somebody's backside in motion above. She turned away but the sobbing continued. Even when she closed her eyes and put her fingers in her ears, she could still hear the sound ringing inside her head. With the days that passed, she took to watching the gate from the window. Repeatedly throughout the day, she would come to the window, draw back the curtains and peer out attentively.

'What are you standing in front of the window for?' Hanan would ask. With a shake of the head, Aliyah quickly retreated.

Aliyah paid little attention to what went on around her. She floated along as though sleep-walking, her toes barely touching the ground. If she ever made a sound, while washing the dishes or polishing the crystal and silverware, she would feel fear seize hold of her and sink into a depression for the rest of the day. Aliyah had taken her own existence and her own self-confidence from where she had found it: within Hanan's body. Before that, she was nothing. After all, wasn't she now capable of making such a rich, beautiful woman happy!

One evening the mistress requested a cup of cinnamon tea. When Aliyah took it to her she found her in the bathtub. The mistress ordered Aliyah to take off her clothes and come closer to help. Then she pulled her into the water, biting her neck until the salty taste touched her tongue. Aliyah was stunned – like a mouse suddenly confronted by a cat – as the mistress continued to kiss her. She was frozen to the spot. The mistress started to kiss the girl's fingers, then she led them wandering to the secret places of her body. When she was completely gratified she whispered a stern order to Aliyah:

'Now leave.'

Only at that moment were her animal instincts roused and Aliyah pounced at her fiercely. Covering her mouth with her hand to stop her screaming, she was victorious in dragging her mistress to the bed. Yet Aliyah's victory ran much deeper than this; she had usurped Hanan, taken her throne – that seat of power founded in violent love or hatred; a vagabond loathing which heeded to nothing.

Aliyah took great delight in the power of her hatred, not suspecting for a moment that Hanan would turn her out onto the streets to be tortured by the hungry flies that bit away at her legs and face. She remembered the day her father had led her through the alleyways and cast her into that house, the House of Colours as she liked to call it. Aliyah resented her mother for sending her all alone to work for the mistress, for not asking after her once in over ten years and, as the days passed, the memories of her mother became tinged with anger and spite. She tried to picture her in the most repulsive way imaginable, but every time only the most beautiful image returned: her mother's faint smile.

Aliyah muttered hoarsely to herself until her voice dissipated in the air. Taking a deep breath, she sensed that her throat was dry. Her gaze turned to the patch of green beneath the tree, settled among the tiny pine needles. She nibbled at her lips, then bit them hard, until she could taste salt.

The silence persisted. Aliyah opened her eyes as wide as they would go. Dazed and obscured, they saw nothing but a roof of green, permeated by beams of violet light. In peaceful surrender, she closed them and leant her head on the bag, her body slipping towards the ground. Sitting beneath the tree, Aliyah surrendered to a sudden sleep. In her dream she vanished behind high walls of green metal. Black bags fell on her head like drops of rain and she shielded her face with her hands. The bags hailed down so hard that she couldn't run away, as the metal walls grew narrower, crushing her between them. Then, rising up from the ground came what seemed at first to be another wall. No, it wasn't a wall; it was a skip. Aliyah screamed at the sight but heard no sound from her voice. She saw two eyes peering out from the shadows, she ran towards them. When she got there the mistress was standing above the two eyes. She fled but Hanan pursued, flying above her head, screeching and howling like the cats of al-Raml. She hid beneath the black sacks, shielding her face from the rotten smells with her hands. Then the bags turned to a sea of rubbish and she began to drown.

Aliyah opened her eyes and woke up from the nightmare. Breathing the air, she exhaled with a deep sigh. Hearing a sobbing sound coming down from the sky above she looked up to see her sister's eyes staring out from the empty space, just as they had that evening.

It wasn't Aboud's face that had caught her attention that evening when she had returned from school to discover him on top of her crippled sister; it was her sister's eyes. That vacant look was just like her mother's as she lay groaning beneath her father's weight. *Why do a woman's eyes turn to empty hollows when she lies beneath a man?*

Despite the darkness, Aliyah could see that her mother was attempting to escape with her eyes, to get far away from her husband's face, as if she were calling for help. Once he had clambered off her mother and she heard the water begin to splutter in the bathroom where her mother was washing, Aliyah always knew that it was time to sleep.

'That's how you make babies,' her little brother said. Aliyah slapped his mouth to keep him quiet, afraid that their father might catch them out and punish them; he would flay their hides with his leather belt, followed by confinement to the bathroom, beside the black pit. That was his most lenient way to admonish them. One night, he had caught her brother spying on him. He dragged him from under the woollen covers where he lay shivering, his teeth chattering with cold and fear. Paying no attention even to the wind that howled between the gaps in the tin sheets that protected the roof, he stripped the boy bare, threw him out into the darkness and locked the door.

At the sound of her brother weeping, Aliyah put her fingers in her ears and closed her eyes beneath the covers. As the crying grew louder, her mother stayed silent, her siblings too, even though they hadn't closed their eyes for a moment. Aliyah couldn't bear the sound any longer. She jumped out of bed, picked up her brother's clothes, which were scattered over the floor, and went out to find him. In the dim light she could barely make out his dark body, which had turned blue. As she attempted to breathe some warmth into his hands her head gave a sudden, violent shake. Barely conscious of what had happened, Aliyah saw stars in her eyes as her father's giant body swooped down to grab hold of her and her brother. He stripped them both bare, before he swung them in his grasp like a pair of mice, slinging them into the bathroom. There, fluorescent red eyes emanated from the deep, black pit. For a few minutes Aliyah fell unconscious, her head hitting the side of the hollow. That pit was where the devils and hyenas came from to steal children, her mother had told her. The creatures kept children trapped in human waste, turning them into tiny insects. As she searched the darkness for her brother, Aliyah heard her mother sobbing, muttering incomprehensibly and smelt the smoke of her father's cigarettes.

The memory was as raw as if it had happened yesterday. Aliyah realised what a paradise she had lost that morning. Lying still beneath the branches of the old pine tree, she hoped this might be her final resting place.

≈

The limbs had begun to grow again – long arms protruding

from below her breasts, wrapping themselves around her, as extra breasts sprouted all over her stomach. Hanan ran down a long, dark corridor then stopped before a full-length mirror. At the sight of her extra arms and breasts in the mirror she screamed, waking up from her few minutes of sleep.

She was still in bed, Hanan discovered, groping at her body. No sign of any extra arms. The persistence of the nightmare's attacks surprised her; why couldn't what she'd seen in her dreams be the end of it? Aliyah naked, on top of her crocodile husband. The image would not leave her mind. Hanan cried, choking on an acid taste as she remembered the girl's dark, gleaming body – the body that she had formed and polished herself – in the arms of a decrepit old crocodile.

Hanan tried to concoct excuses for the maid who had given her so much happiness.

'I told her to follow his orders.'

But what orders? I wanted her to feed him and make him drinks, and to change his sheets before they were soaked with his rancid sweat, not to lie in his arms.

'Maybe he made her do it,' Hanan tried to convince herself, knowing full well that her husband's only activity was to await death. She herself knew that wait intimately; she had witnessed it with the death of her mother and uncles. A hereditary weakness flowed in the family blood. Hanan knew it, but was no longer worried. Perhaps she never had been worried, really. The way she saw it, death meant release and, in a way, she was waiting too. She had forgotten that though, once Nazek had helped her to discover those secret realms of pleasure, once she had become consumed by passion for the servant girl. The girl who, at night, would hear her own bones crack as she panted above the old man, tirelessly licking his skin.

Hanan's limbs had turned numb with anxiety. She needed to sleep but feared the dream she might find herself in. Descending the stairs once more, she rushed to the full-length mirror, just like before. She turned on the light and looked fixedly at the pallid face before her, stroking her cheeks. The old woman in the mirror had black rings around her eyes. Her small head rested on bony shoulders and her short hair stood on end, like iron needles. Hanan ruffled her hair. It stayed just as it was. Her face was comical, like the moving images of a cartoon.

Hanan figured she must still be dreaming, otherwise how would her hair stay looking so ridiculous, like a hedgehog? She took a few steps away from the mirror and turned full circle, checking there were no protrusions growing from her body. She stopped, coiling from the pain in her stomach. As she imagined the details of her maid's body she felt a deadly jealousy. Every pore, scar, mole and hair, she remembered clearly. Each curve, the roundness of her breasts, the arching of her buttocks, the rise of her backside, her long thighs, she knew every bit of the girl's body by heart, down to the glint in her eyes, which frightened her sometimes when their roles reversed. Hanan had preserved every detail. Yet, for the first time, as she stared into the mirror, she realised that the long years which she had shared with Aliyah had been empty of conversation. In the daytime, Aliyah was silent. She acknowledged her orders with a gentle nod, the only word ever to come from her voice being 'ma'am'.

This one word was all that remained of Aliyah's voice. Hanan was surprised by her late discovery, racking her brain for any memory of a conversation between them, attempting to recapture the girl's sound. But it was no use.

Hanan's mobile was ringing from inside her room. She

wondered who would be calling her at that time. She dragged herself upstairs, afraid to answer, yet equally curious to know who it was calling so early.

When she got to the phone, the ringing had stopped. It was Nazek, who waited no time before ringing again. Hanan peered fearfully at the phone. Nazek would send her insane; she would discover her secret, and she might gloat at her misfortune.

The phone continued to ring. Hanan picked it up and threw it.

She tried to get a grasp of what she should do to bring Aliyah back. All the while, Nazek's voice rang out in her head. She recalled its rasping tone, as she had heard it the evening of Nazek's gathering in honour of Caroline, the artist who was her new lover, even though she was still chasing Hanan.

'One last glass,' Nazek had rasped, pouring Hanan her favourite vodka. She drew so close that her bosom almost grazed Hanan's chin. As she looked directly into her eyes, Nazek poured the vodka down Hanan's front, laughing as Hanan yelped at the chilling ice. Leaning towards her damp body, she kissed Hanan on the lips, savouring the scent. Hanan ignored Nazek's burning glances and fixed her sight on the two women sprawled on the sofa nearby.

'Are you afraid, my little sparrow?' Nazek queried, starting to cackle again.

Hanan made no comment. Caroline and Fatima were a world away, staring into each other's eyes. As she observed the women, they drew closer together, their lips not quite touching, but no more than a hair's width apart. This was a strange place, she thought. Even though Hanan had accompanied

Nazek on many evenings, at this one she really felt she was in another world. Perhaps it was because she was so taken with Aliyah, or because she had noticed Nazek trying to get close to another woman. Or maybe it was the giant candles that Nazek had placed on all four sides of the room, lit in three-tiered spirals. Nazek had taken to collecting candles from all over the world and paid great sums of money for them. Disliking the feel of electric lighting in the evenings, instead she dotted candles throughout every metre of her desert mansion. Yet that evening, she lit only a few, wanting forms to be obscured, to stop the walls from turning to peering eyes. Portraits by great painters, which hung on the walls, were driven to distraction in Nazek's possession, having to sit with her those long hours as she drank her coffee and stared at them admiringly. Even though she loved her expensive paintings and the great ivory sculptures dotted about the corners of the house, Nazek chose to cloak them all in shadow.

Despite the low light, Hanan could still make out a new chaise longue in Nazek's collection. The elongated seat, a yellowish red colour, came close to the side of a bed. Its legs were plated with ivory, the fabric was striped gold and silver and the back of the seat was curved like a violin. On one end was a long supporting arm while the other was open, like a royal carriage.

Hanan pictured Aliyah stretched out on the seat before her. The vision sent a shudder running through her body. She was sure she felt sadder than before, daydreaming of Aliyah. When she noticed her favourite white roses, Hanan realised what great trouble Nazek had gone to for her. There were white carnations, white irises, damask roses, lilies and jasmine too, all white. But none were of any use in attracting Hanan's attention, or in winning the heart she had left at home with Aliyah. Hanan was suffocating with desire for her servant. She began moving drunkenly, peering about her. If only she could keep still. Yet she knew her body wouldn't lie to her; she wasn't the woman she had once been.

Hanan was barely aware of what was happening around her. She wanted to fly far away, to find out, as she spun around laughing with her eyes closed, who would still be there when she got dizzy. What would be left? Aliyah's fingers? Nazek's lips?

Her head seemed a tiny dot sinking far away in an ocean, having separated from her body. Like a drowning person, she was dreaming of reaching the lowest ring of the whirlpool. If it hadn't been for Nazek, who ran to catch her, Hanan's head would have hit the floor. Nazek dragged her to the chaise longue and held her tightly to her chest, patting her cheeks gently.

'Hanan, my darling,' she whispered.

Hanan was unable to hear her and Nazek had the unbearable feeling that she was slipping away. As Caroline turned on the lights, they saw Hanan's pale face peering at Nazek, whose infatuation was quite apparent, expressed clearly in the icy way she had greeted her. Nazek found herself unable in that moment to give Hanan any sort of guidance. It wasn't the first time that a lover had abandoned her. Some had wanted to marry; others only stayed with her a night or two, simply to keep her happy. Some would even end up as regular guests. But Hanan was of another sort; she had given her body out of desire, not for some other benefit. This Nazek knew, and she valued Hanan for it. Her attachment grew stronger until she began to organise her whole life around the finer points of Hanan's desires.

Nazek took hold of Hanan's fingers and started to rub them. She took off Hanan's shoes and lifted her legs, lying her down. Placing Hanan's head in her lap, she sat teary-eyed as she gently stroked her forehead and examined the lines of pain appearing in her expression. Caroline and Fatima stood observing, affected by the scene. Suddenly Caroline burst into tears.

'What a miserable state we're all in,' she stuttered, pouring herself another glass, which she left aside. The magic of the evening had gone for good.

'I'm scared,' Fatima said, biting her nails as her eyes darted about her as though she were looking out for a murderer. Caroline put her arms around Fatima's shoulders and stole a kiss, to which Fatima made no response. Her eyes were fixed on Hanan, who had started to stir. Nazek had placed an arm around Hanan to help her to sit up and when Hanan slowly opened her eyes, she breathed a sigh of relief. She was on her way back from another world, and felt as though not a single moment of her life already passed bore any relation to her now. She gazed at Nazek, searching for a familiar face, as Caroline wasted no time in asking what had happened.

Nazek clapped her hands.

'Let's have some coffee.' Hanan nodded in agreement and Nazek got up to make the coffee since, as usual, the servants had left before the evening had begun. Fatima and Caroline began to whisper once more, their voices rising and falling. With her hands clutching Fatima's face, Caroline spoke.

'I promise that won't happen to you. I won't let you come to any harm. Whatever happens now will quickly be over. Marry him. I know what you have to go through every time they see you with me. Marry him; I'll be happy with whatever happens. I'll be by your side.'

'Do you really mean it?'

'Absolutely. We'll still see each other. Just promise you'll stay with me. We can keep it all secret, trust me.'

The scent of coffee filled the room, stirring Hanan from her drowsiness. Caroline and Fatima were deeply absorbed in their kiss, as though each were trying to fuse with the other. Quietly, they retreated to the next-door bedroom. Hanan remained silent as she sipped her coffee, Nazek watching her attentively.

'Do you feel better?'

Hanan nodded as Nazek lit her a cigarette. The silence was heavy. Even the noises coming from the bedroom were barely audible. They weren't the sounds of desire, more those of a dying animal. The unsettling sound, which was accompanied by soft cries, made Hanan begin to tremble once more. She asked Nazek to take her up to the second floor. Nazek took Hanan by the hand and led her to the staircase like a lost child. Slowly, they ascended, Nazek turning every few steps to give her a furtive kiss, on the lips, on the neck, over her eyes. Hanan laughed and bit Nazek in return, responding to her affection without much feeling. Perhaps what she had heard of Caroline and Fatima's conversation had made her jealous. Nazek was eager to satisfy her own burning desires; there was a certain violence in her caresses, a force which betrayed her own feeling that she couldn't hold on to Hanan.

The mirror shone. The phone was still ringing. Hanan did not answer. Stroking her neck, she remembered the imprints Nazek's kisses had left that night and her sadness grew deeper, confirming her belief that the matter of her feelings had been decided in Aliyah's favour. She recalled the chaise longue which she had asked Nazek about, hoping that one day she might buy it for her lover. Hanan was angry with herself for expelling the girl. *What harm was there in her sucking an old crocodile's skin? Wasn't she still more faithful than Nazek, who had always insisted she be one of several girlfriends?*

～

The heat of the sun was growing stronger and sweat mingled with the dust covering Aliyah's body as she heaved her bag along, limping like a wounded animal. The clammy moisture gathered over her forehead, beneath her clothes and on her scalp. After living in squalor the first half of her life, the second half she had spent in such comfort that the clammy feeling was unbearable to her now.

Those games in the bathtub gave Aliyah a joy like no other. Even when they became daily routine, none of the happiness was lost. She would rub her mistress's back and massage her whole body, discovering the beauty of her own dark complexion in contrast with the mistress's fairness, a sight which caught her attention as the water glistened over her skin and the steam opened her pores. Aliyah felt great pleasure in sensing her mistress's desires. Sometimes she dared to strip off and bathe first, filling the white bathtub with water, perfumed oils and dried rose petals, just as her mistress had taken to doing. As she studied her image in the bathroom mirror, she discovered that she had changed completely; Aliyah was no more. Once she had slipped into the tub and closed her eyes, the mistress would follow and their roles would be reversed; Hanan would massage her body as she contemplated her firm breasts, sketching lines on her thighs. Then she would dry her with a warm towel and lead her to her bed. Aliyah felt so safe there that the damage done by the horrors of nights in al-Raml was repaired. She began to feel she was never born there, that the mistress had fashioned her from the embryo of her desire.

Aliyah closed her eyes to the road and, rather than car fumes, she smelt cinnamon. The scent made her delirious – that same fragrance which had filled the air as her mistress's fingers took over her own and guided them. In complete innocence Aliyah's fingers drew the scent across Hanan's body. With her eyes closed, the fragrance led Hanan into a stupor. She sensed that her grip on the reins was lost; Aliyah had taken hold of her entirely, from the soles of her feet to the very top of her head. She seized hold of the girl's fingers, croaking at her to stop. Then, slumping, she looked into her eyes.

'That's my girl,' she said to herself.

Aliyah took a deep breath; the excess of desire had brought her to the brink of suffocation. She should have found consolation in her recollections, but now she felt frightened. Frightened of the scent. Frightened of the touch of silk in a world that was no longer hers. She had to prepare herself to return to her former life, the one she thought she had left behind forever.

Expelled from her paradise, Aliyah wandered alone in space. She fondled the sharp knife concealed beneath her clothes. The first time her mistress had taken advantage of her this was that same knife she had immediately sought. She would strangle her, she thought, as the mistress towered above. She would bite her; she would tear her to shreds, just as she had the boys of al-Raml. Yet pleasure was more desirable than resistance. She couldn't resist those caresses, which made her feel something bubbling up inside her, turning her into an animal needing to bite.

Now she was capable of devouring men and women equally, with the same desire and strength, Aliyah thought. She had learnt it all! She muttered to herself, still walking along the road. She knew how to be patient in waiting for what she wanted. That was exactly what she had done until the mistress became the pawn of her desires and the master a slave to his servant's games. She had turned the grand house into her own palace where others could be made to move according to her will. Daytimes were of little importance; she could clean more or less as she fancied, since Hanan no longer held her to account for anything. But at night things were different. She no longer had use for her knife; all that she needed was a few new games to play with Hanan. Aliyah shivered at the thought of Hanan's caresses, having never forgotten the night she had held on to her, dangling her as she swung between her thighs. She stopped for a minute, placing her hand on her forehead as her vision became immersed in the endless road before her. For a second her sight went. Then she walked on once more, almost in a zigzag. She panted with exhaustion.

Aliyah didn't feel happy. She wasn't sad either. She felt nothing extraordinary, other than that it was the first time that any being had overwhelmed her with such love. She hadn't thought to question whether her actions were lawful or sinful. She had begun waiting for the evenings, when Hanan would silently call for her. The mistress's looks alone would tell her what was going to happen. Often she would start to caress Hanan without her showing the slightest interest, but as soon as she turned to meet her eyes, Aliyah would understand what she wanted. This was how it proceeded until one day when the mistress came back to the house late at night, whilst Aliyah was asleep. Hanan entered her room, whistling a sad tune. She woke Aliyah up, took her to her own room and had sex with her. The girl soon fell asleep, not to wake until morning when the cook knocked at the door. Hanan was startled to see Aliyah lying next to her as she heard the knocking on the door and noticed the sun exposing her naked body in scandalous detail. The cook waited behind the door until Hanan ordered her to leave. Hanan peered at the stunned expression on Aliyah's face, which turned a lemon colour when confronted with the mistress's terrifying look of rage.

Aliyah stood naked before Hanan. The mistress waved her hands wildly, cursing and swearing as she scrambled about the room in search of something to cover her body, all the while beating her aching head. Aliyah moved not an inch from her spot, but stood frozen, clueless as to what was happening. What had provoked her mistress's anger? What had she possibly done wrong? She had no idea, until the mistress screamed:

'How could you have let yourself stay in my bed until morning?'

Aliyah gazed perplexed at her crazed mistress and scrambled off the bed. As she pulled on her clothes, she felt her eyes welling up, as if about to erupt. Retreating from the room to her own, she locked the door behind her, threw herself onto the bed and started to sob loudly, that animal viciousness stirring inside her.

From that moment on, Aliyah would make the mistress pay a heavy price for humiliating her, she decided, but with a method that wouldn't force her to leave the house forever and become a beggar getting fucked by other beggars.

Aliyah started to mess with Anwar, brushing past him on purpose, bending over him to pick something up from by his side or to open the curtains. She would spend a few minutes cleaning his bathroom, then come out half-naked, humming loudly. Anwar would open his eyes and remain frozen as he watched her move about his bedroom. When Aliyah could sense his eyes on her, she would start to make strange noises like a cat's miaul – sounds she had learnt in her mistress's arms. At other times, she would intentionally trip over his feet, then sigh and apologise, and tenderly smooth his clothes. She would gyrate her behind with delight as his chin rocked with pleasure and he stared at her in silent alarm. Yet he did not remain like this for long, since the maid was capable of reviving the faded voice of his masculinity.

Aliyah's efforts bore fruit in returning to Anwar a part of his strength. She continued her games, not merely as an act of revenge against Hanan, but because the idea of mounting both master and mistress, of toying with them both, pleased her. In one day she would make the mistress sit before her on all fours, then later play with the master in the same way. Aliyah simply continued her games, which never went beyond the bed – the only place where she had ever felt that she was queen.

When she got out of bed in the morning, Aliyah would stand before her mirror, staring at her own face. She would take hold of the end of her chin and raise it upwards and, with a smile, place one hand on her shoulder, as though wearing a sash and holding herself erect.

'Lady Aliyah!' she repeated aloud.

Aliyah turned towards the door. 'The day's begun,' she said. At night she would continue to rule in both beds, on both floors of the villa, with only a trivial difference. When she was with Anwar, it was he who stayed silent whilst she chattered on, particularly once she had begun to sense her own power.

With Hanan, things were a little different; Aliyah had taken to silence, knowing how much it tortured her. She no longer displayed any sign in her movements; neither of indifference nor love. Their relationship was closer to a battle, a vengeful coup that was Aliyah's response to the betrayal Hanan had announced on one occasion far from her bed. But then, unlike now, Hanan hadn't thrown her out on the street.

After Hanan had turfed her from her bed, Aliyah stopped responding to her night-time calls. Eventually Hanan gave up hope and took to sleeping the whole day. One evening, the room bell rang. Aliyah jumped at the sound, gripped by a surprising chill. She bounded out of bed, opened the door and tiptoed out. Normally, she would open Hanan's door without knocking, but this time she lingered until she heard Hanan's voice croak from inside the room.

'Open the door.'

Aliyah entered and stepped towards the bed. The mistress was lying on her back and Aliyah could see nothing but her gaze, burning bright like a cat's eyes on a dark night. Sensing a ghostly figure brush against her skin, she stood shaking.

'Scared?' Hanan cackled.

As Hanan reached out her hand, Aliyah surrendered, the mistress gently pulling her closer. Aliyah wanted to strike her, to attack her with her knife and then leave the villa forever. Yet instead, she yielded.

There was one particular moment which Aliyah remembered, and which she would continue to recall for a long time to come. As she was recollecting the long conversations on those cold winter evenings about women humiliated by men, how Suzuki had once humiliated her and how Aboud had brought shame on her sister, Aliyah had felt as though her body were unfurling into strange protrusions. And in that instant she recognised all of those things that had happened for what they were. She had no desire to do the same herself, yet this was the only way for her to make her own way, to create her own games. Aliyah kissed her mistress ferociously and, just her father had forced himself on her mother, she now did the same. She threw Hanan down and mounted her, an act that gave her a feeling of power. Hanan cried out, staring fixedly at her maid but Aliyah didn't let up. From the verge of rage, Hanan's anger turned into sighs and moans, punctuating Aliyah's movements as she kissed her mistress's body and bit her flesh. Under the control of her lust and the pain she felt, Aliyah was unaware of what she had done. She was waiting for her mistress to stop shaking and screaming, so she could do it again.

Hanan was teetering on the point of sweet exhaustion. The servant girl had changed for good, she knew it. Too late to win her back. Although she assented to the maid's violence, Hanan still cried out to her each night, hoping to catch a glimpse of tenderness in the girl's vicious eyes. But as her mistress was becoming all the more affectionate and submissive, Aliyah's maliciousness was strengthening.

The night before, Aliyah had abandoned Hanan in deep sleep. She took a long cigarette from the supply that Hanan kept as a treat for her, lit it and went back to her room, exhaling the smoke as she stood in front of the window. Aliyah drew back the net curtains. The place was in darkness and, except for the soft glow of the garden lights, it seemed there was no world beyond the walls of the house. She drew slowly on the cigarette, like she'd seen women in films do, absorbed in their illicit pleasure.

'These pleasures are yours – you deserve them,' she told herself. 'The filthy alleys of al-Raml are far behind you now.'

With one hand on her hip, Aliyah span around like a ballet dancer, drawing the cigarette close to her eyes.

'You're the woman in charge around here,' she whispered.

Aliyah had started to gnaw at the heavy cigarette. She moved towards the window and drew back the curtains, bending forward a little to lean out of the window. Aliyah took a long breath, then stood up and tip-toed back across the room.

'Lady Aliyah, the day will never break again; everything you see is under your command.'

Aliyah headed down towards the master's bedroom, where Anwar was snoring loudly, oblivious to the creak of the door as she entered, closing the door behind her. In silence, she slid in beside him and stripped off her clothes. Anwar stirred peacefully and turned towards her. Realising that the vision before him was true, Anwar sat up, his gaze devouring her body. With a shudder, he backed away. Aliyah drew herself closer in silence, clinging to his body and twisting her own as she lay in his arms. A few stammered words fell from Anwar's lips as beads of sweat slid over his forehead, gathering at the base of his back. Aliyah did not know what she had said, that had almost caused him to fall on the floor as he fled to the farthest part of the bed and she followed.

'You deserve everything you get,' Aliyah chastised herself, holding back a tear which glistened in the corner of her eye. She recalled how Anwar had been so frightened of her that he fell out of the bed. Aliyah wiped away the tear and continued onwards, stumbling from the weight of her bag.

∼

Another ring. The house phone this time.

It had to be Nazek. She must have given up on her answering her mobile. Hanan reached out her hand for the receiver and thought about asking her to come over, or perhaps just crying into the phone. She hesitated. She could ask Nazek to help her to look for Aliyah. Nazek could do anything.

The phone stopped ringing. From behind the curtains, the sun had launched its attack on the room. The streak of light that had turned her life to a nightmare had vanished beneath the rays of sunlight dancing in the air. Hanan decided not to pick up.

She went out onto the balcony, breathing in a little fresh air and watching the flocks of birds. Hanan's heart jolted beneath her ribs. She remembered the illuminated patch of ground at the base of Mount Qasyoun, where the cooing pigeons gathered. The gardener had started to cut the grass in the villa garden and the noise startled the birds, who scattered in every direction, leaving just a single flock to hover over the place. Hanan breathed softly as she remembered the days when she would watch the pigeons from her partially open window. Perhaps she should concentrate on the flock of birds, on anything that might take her mind off Aliyah.

In those days, Damascus winters were white, not cloaked in black. The rain would run from the foot of Qasyoun, passing beside the stone staircase and beneath Hanan's window. Hanan loved to hear the roar of the water, especially as she went to sleep. She would listen to it beating against the side of the house, great droplets hitting the glass of the window. As she wrapped herself up in her covers, she felt happy and refreshed, as if sleeping on a cloud.

Hanan was fifteen years old and still learning how to be a woman from the girls at school, from her trips to the public baths and the women's coffee mornings in Damascus. Hanan's mother had never taught her the art of femininity; she simply gave orders and expected to be obeyed. She went to the most well-respected seamstresses to commission the most beautiful dresses for her only daughter, whom she would force to accompany her on her visits to other families. She would never forget to tell the women what great lengths she'd gone to for her daughter's dress to look just so; she had had the dress made to order so that it would be unique. Then she had taken it to a special embroiderer, and afterwards gone round all of the seamstresses one by one, until she was convinced that she had found the right design – exactly what she had in mind. Even though she had her own seamstress, she had wanted to have something particularly special made for her daughter, she told the women, who were growing weary as they listened jealously. As she spoke, she would order Hanan to stand and parade around in front of them, to demonstrate the beauty of the new style on her. Hanan was always quick to obey her mother, with a dignity beyond her years. Her obedience was another source of jealousy to the other mothers, who wished their daughters were as well-behaved as Hanan al-Hashimi.

Hanan was her family's pride and joy, attracting the enchanted gazes of others. As she grew older, she learnt to use their eyes as a mirror. Eyes ready to be dazzled by her presence. Yet those Damascus mornings when she opened her window and the rain had stopped falling were among the few instances when Hanan felt out-of-place. She focused on a spot of sky stealing through the gaps between the leaves of the Quina trees lining the pavement. The sight of the white pigeons hopping from one roof to another took her heart even further away. There was nothing more beautiful than the sight of a cooing pigeon in the Damascus sky, rising up to Qasyoun, and then soaring back down to the neighbouring houses.

One day as Hanan was sitting in her room watching the white pigeons, her mother opened the door. She stood in the doorway, rubbing her fingers with uncharacteristic worry. As she entered the room, Hanan closed the window and the birds vanished.

'How are your studies?' her mother asked.

'Fine,' Hanan replied succinctly, her hoarse voice trembling.

Hanan's mother spent no time skirting around what she had come to tell her daughter; she was to marry her cousin. Hanan was speechless. How could she possibly marry Anwar? The man she'd grown up with as his little sister. As her mother sat down beside her on the bed, Hanan backed away and went to open the window. A cold breeze blew into the room and gave her mother a chill. Hanan stood motionless in front of the window, her hair dancing in the wind. She thought about how Anwar had divorced his first wife only a month ago and how the news had worried the family, who so badly wanted a child to ensure the family's future. The matter had made the family quite restless, since Anwar refused to marry again. Hanan had heard the fights between Anwar and her uncle, but was excluded from knowing the family business. Even if she had an interest in what was being said, nobody would listen to her.

Hanan was certain there must have been some mistake, but she wasn't in the habit of discussing matters, nor was she used to opposing her mother's will. She hadn't expected – and certainly couldn't imagine – that Anwar, her big brother, could become her husband. Hanan fell silent, leaving her mother's decision unchallenged. Her mother drew towards her and patted her on the shoulder.

'Nothing will change,' she said. 'You'll just have to move rooms, to Anwar's. You can continue your studies. That I promise.'

At that moment, Hanan turned towards her mother and stared directly at her, her own expression sketched with bewilderment. She couldn't stay silent; the self-control that her mother had trained her to employ with others was powerless now. Tears welled in Hanan's eyes.

'I can't!' she sobbed.

In a rare moment of tenderness, Hanan's mother put her arms around her shoulders and began playing with her daughter's hair.

'Don't be scared,' she whispered. 'Nothing's going to change. All you have to do is move into Anwar's room. We'll still be together, and the family will be complete again. You'll become a whole woman. It won't be difficult.'

How could it not be difficult? Hanan stared unfalteringly at her mother. Her mind strayed to thoughts of Anwar and his wife, who had departed the family's life a few months before. Hanan had been happy in her own little world, the one within the walls of her bedroom. She hadn't asked why her cousin had returned. In the evenings, as she sat embroidering her white cloth with pictures of birds, windows and daisies, she heard them talking. The family would disintegrate if Anwar didn't marry again, and their lives would change if he did, with his insistence that his wife was not at fault. None of this had meant a thing to Hanan before, but that was different now. She couldn't possibly accept that the man who had been a brother to her would become her husband. Her body shuddered at the word, and her skin crawled. Exhausted, Hanan sat on the bed, the pores of her trembling skin filling with soft pimples. She watched the lips as they opened and closed, a loud drone ringing in her ears, followed by silence. Hanan could no longer hear what her mother was saying. Her head was on fire. She closed her eyes and became submerged in slumber.

Hanan wasn't sure what had happened after that. Anwar disappeared without her even seeing him. Everything was arranged as she lay in her bed greeting developments with languid gestures of approval. In the run-up to the wedding Anwar persistently entered her thoughts with the one unforgettable image she held of him: Anwar the big brother she'd always dreamt of. His soft hands stroked her hair. He and his wife gave her morsels of food, treating her like their daughter. Hanan remembered too the wonderful trips they had taken to Bloudan and Zabadani, how the couple had spoilt her like a puppy dog. She had never recalled those details before, so why now? It must be God's way of torturing her for having revolted against her mother, and for hating her so. That must be the reason.

Hanan asked her mother to stay with her constantly, to fend off the memories which returned like nightmares. The family interpreted her distress as a bride's fear of her big night. There were only a few days to go until the wedding, which they had arranged to be very special: the celebrations would pervade the whole district of Muhajireen, and would last several days. Hanan saw little of the party, however. Through the closed window, she heard the dances and *dabkeh* parties going on in the nearby street. The window had stayed shut since she had closed it, at noon on that day when she had watched the flock of pigeons playing in the busy sky, amongst the branches of the quinine trees.

Hanan refused to go to the women's bathhouse. It was the one form of resistance she could muster before her family, a clear message that she wanted to throw herself from Mount Qasyoun and tumble down between the white stone houses. She would rather burn in hell than have to touch that man, whom she loathed now more than anyone. The mere recollection of the bathhouse, of the fluttering shiver she had enjoyed as a child sitting in the neighbour's lap, was enough to make her feel all the more wretched. Instead, Hanan chose to wash as if it were an ordinary day. Then, she left her room to watch the servants moving her clothes and other possessions into Anwar's new quarters. She and her mother entered the room. Her white dress was pulled tight around her waist, her face covered with a soft white veil, embellished with lace and sparkling white pearls. Hanan hadn't thought about the imminent pain; the usual fear of a girl approaching her wedding night did not even enter her mind. She knew that women had been created to bear pain, as her mother had told her. The best thing to do was to endure it silently, to resist it with stoicism, equanimity and composure.

Hanan closed her eyes and turned off the lights. She sat on the edge of the bed, like an actress in an Egyptian film. She waited. And waited. Anwar too was hoping it wouldn't have to happen. Yet he had surrendered, along with his cousin, feeling an inescapable sense of loyalty to his family with the painful recognition that he was the last remaining male. This sense of allegiance made the situation easier for him. Anwar entered his wife's room without turning on the lights. He stopped and waited, gazing at what he could make out of her white dress beneath the faint streaks of light coming in through the window. In the darkness, there was a sense of collusion between Anwar and Hanan, and until Anwar took hold of his bride's hand to kiss it everything was fine. Once he had pulled her close and sensed her shaking Anwar could no longer contain himself. He patted her forehead, just as he had always done when she was a little girl, when she would sit in his lap twirling his moustache and playing with his cheeks. There was a familiar scent; the scent of infants, he realised. Anwar drew away from his cousin and pulled back the curtains to dispel the last of the shadows, so that her image would vanish from before him.

That evening Hanan came of age. She said goodbye to her old world and slipped skilfully and silently into the responsibilities of her new routine. Whenever her mother asked how her husband was treating her – whether he was kind and cordial – Hanan made no response. Her mother interpreted this as shyness, dropping the subject until much later when Hanan began asking for advice on how to gain her husband's affections in the bedroom. Her daughter's exclamation that her husband wanted to bite her lips and nibble at her breasts frightened her. The girl was incomplete, she felt. These were the signs of corners cut in her training to becoming a good wife, of an over-emphasis on decorum. Hanan's instruction was of no use to her in dealing with her fear of the evenings, which increased as the years passed and she did not become pregnant. Anwar had started to keep his distance, not just from her but from the house altogether. He hadn't noticed how she had engrossed herself in completing her studies, in keeping up with her mother and the neighbours, going to her parties and fulfilling her other duties. She continued with her studies because it was what her mother wanted; it was for her sake that she stayed at home. To Hanan, it didn't matter; there was no life running through her veins. It was as if she'd been born dead, as if she'd been created simply to march towards death. Hanan had a destructive urge to slip into a coma and be relieved of the burdens of her world, as if she had never existed. As if she had never been her mother's daughter.

What would have happened if she had refused Anwar point blank? She wondered now.

The telephone rang once more and stirred Hanan from her daydreams. She went back inside and shut the curtains, as if to hide from it. The room was bathed in darkness. Hanan felt calmer. She pulled the telephone cord out from the wall and, with trembling hands, switched off her mobile, throwing it to the ground. As Hanan lay on her bed exhausted, Nazek's face appeared before her. She had tortured Nazek so badly, she thought. Nazek had done so much to please her and to win her back from that pock-marked maid, the maid who, when all was said and done, was her little lover.

~

Hanan's little lover gave up all hope of the rubbish truck coming, or of spotting anyone walking through the place, which was silent even though the sun had now risen towards the domed roof of the sky. Aliyah's mind was in another place – the place where she belonged, where she could remove her veneers and return to her mother's embrace, to be just as she was created. She wouldn't let life pass her by anymore, Aliyah reassured herself. She would do all sorts of things.

The heel of her shoe snapped instantly as Aliyah stamped in anger, assuring herself that she was going to be ok. She fell. She turned her head to look back. Why she felt a sharp twinge in her chest as she imagined her old world had disappeared, as though it had never existed, she did not know.

Taking off her shoes, Aliyah found the source of her troubles. A small tack had come loose. This was a problem she could resolve. She put her bag aside, picked up a stone and bashed the tack back into the heel. Putting on the shoes, which fastened around her ankles, she cautiously set off once more. Why hadn't she brought any other shoes? Pausing, Aliyah realised something: they weren't her shoes! They were Hanan's.

Aliyah tried to recollect what shoes she had worn in Hanan's house and laughed; she realised she'd never had a pair to leave the house in. The only shoes she had were special ones for the house – footwear for service. Even on the rare occasions when she was obliged to go out, Aliyah wore the same shoes. The thought hadn't entered Hanan's mind to buy her any, even though she had showered her with presents and even taught her how to smoke. Aliyah was a prisoner; a slave to the whims of her mistress, who wanted her never to go beyond the villa walls.

She carried on her way, dreaming of her mother's room. Things would be better once she got to al-Raml, she tried to reassure herself. Suddenly, a figure appeared in the distance. Her heart jumped and she ran towards it. A moment later, she realised she was hallucinating; her discovery was nothing but a disappointing trick causing her to take off again. Remembering Anwar lying naked in his room, Aliyah felt pity. She frowned. He had been so happy waiting for her to come to him on those long nights. She could sense his longing, the joy he felt when she skirted by him while cleaning, when he pretended to be sleeping or when seemed to be afraid as she undressed in his room, all the while ignoring his servile glances. Anwar's image drew closer. That final image. His body's odour. Aliyah felt nauseous and started to wretch once more.

The mistress's scent allowed Aliyah to flourish – to open out and grow taller, while the master's made her feel the need to wash at the end of the evening. *Why do it with him then? Why destroy your life with your own hands?* Aliyah shrugged and carried on along the road, away from Hanan.

~

Hanan awoke from her brief doze and looked towards the window. It was as if a mountain were weighing over her head. For a second she forgot who she was. She groped at her chest, finding no additional breasts. Ants were crawling beneath her skin; she could feel them nibbling away at her heart. But when she looked at her hands there was no sign of the insects. Hanan burst into tears.

She opened her window out onto the green plain and the little palaces with their rendered facades. Thinking of Aliyah – of her startled little face – Hanan felt her love was stronger than ever before. She pictured Aliyah's tall frame as the girl walked alone. Fire sparked in her chest as she recalled the look of Aliyah's teary eyes.

Hanan ran out without putting on her headscarf, paying no attention to the gardener cutting back the trees. It wasn't until she felt the sharp pebbles below that she noticed her feet were bare. Heading straight for the car, Hanan realised she wasn't carrying her keys and ran back even wilder this time, panting as she made her way up to the top floor. Quickly, she emptied her leather bag, grabbed hold of the keys, descended the stairs and got into the car.

Bewildered, the gardener ran to open the great iron gate, yet to his surprise it was already unlocked. Strange; he was sure he'd pulled the bolt over before going to bed, but the mistress was driving at such speed there was little time for him to think. He ran towards the house, sure that something must have happened for her to be going out barefoot in her thin nightdress, with untamed hair and bloodshot eyes. The master must be dead. The gardener dashed to Anwar's room, surprised to find him standing behind the window, barely able to support himself. Leaning on his ivory cane, Anwar's emotionless gaze followed Hanan. He paid not the slightest attention as the gardener greeted him. Anwar remained so still that for a second the gardener imagined his master had turned to stone; his eyelashes made not the slightest flutter as he stared with eyes startlingly wide.

Hanan drove at high-speed, her heart pounding. She surveyed the place around her but found no trace of Aliyah. She ventured down every side street and each of the mansion driveways, turning around each time to leave a cloud of dust and disappointment in her wake. The silence of the road was alarming. Hanan was scared as she looked about her, watching out for any sign of another living being, lest someone discover her humiliated state. The residents of the area had all chosen to build out of Damascus to keep their secrets private and to enjoy the fresh air. There in their odd-shaped mansions, with their tiled swimming pools and wide tennis courts, they were far from prying neighbours, from news of the scandals they might be exposed to.

Hanan went from street to street. Aliyah must have got further than she thought. In the distance, she spotted a group of dogs gathering around the remains of an animal. Hanan felt uneasy. She locked the car door and turned down another side-street. Aliyah must be hiding behind one of the walls, she convinced herself as she turned the steering wheel, chewing on her lip. Joy glimmered in Hanan's eyes as she drove around some of the houses. She stopped when she came to the open ground and the long road that separated the cluster of mansions from the first villa standing alone. The land stretched out for miles, the whole space illuminated by the light of the sun. Hanan got out of the car and glanced about her as if getting ready to dance.

The place was empty but for the flocks of birds in the distance.

'Aliyah!' Hanan shouted. The voice was loud. She didn't feel as if it were hers. She called out again, but there was no response. No voice calling out in harmony.

Hanan got into her car and set off at speed, startling a pigeon, which took off high into the sky as she careered away, leaving in her wake a thick cloud of dust.